Double Danger

by

Mary Ann Kerl

Double Danger

Cover Art by *Jennifer Greeff*

The Wild Rose Press, Inc.
PO Box 708
Adams Basin, NY 14410-0708
Visit us at www.thewildrosepress.com

Publishing History
First Edition, 2023
Trade Paperback ISBN 978-1-5092-5019-6
Digital ISBN 978-1-5092-5020-2

Published in the United States of America

Sonny gave a huge wheeze, slammed his fists on the steering wheel and glared at Allen. "We forgot to set the bomb for an hour later. Why'd you forget such a thing?"

"Why'd you forget?" Allen snapped back.

Slowly, Sonny exhaled, leaned back on the seat, closed his eyes and whispered, "Wait a minute, dummy. What're we arguin' fer?" He opened his eyes and grinned.

Allen groaned. "I don't see what there is to smile about."

"Think! It'll still go off, just later is all."

Allen started laughing.

"Shhhhhhh, dude, keep it down. We don't want anyone to hear us."

"Right, Boss Man. Right. Only twenty-five minutes before the fireworks."

Sonny snickered as he did the gang hand symbol with Allen. "That'll give us just enough time to get outta here so we don't get hurt. Then we can come back later to see the damage we caused. If Melody and Jordan are still alive, we'll have to take 'em down."

Allen snickered. "I love the way ya' think, Boss Man."

Praise

Double Danger is double the fun with dynamic action and deadpan humor along the lines of writers Ben Rehder and MC Beaton. You won't want to quit turning the pages as you follow Melody's and Jordan's search for dangerous escaped convicts and the truth about their feelings for one another.

~Karen Whalen, author

~*~

Ms. Kerl writes with clarity and emotion, and weaves romance into a story of danger as her characters overcoming life-threatening events.

~Colleen Norman, author

~*~

Double Danger stays true to the title from beginning to conclusion. It immerses the reader at the outset in a heart thumping prison riot and describes the characters in an authentic way. If you like action, intrigue, and romance you will enjoy this novel. Mary Ann Kerl, author, started strong and finished strong.

~ Brent Brantley, author (former law enforcement) of You Cannot Grasp the River.

Dedication

This book is dedicated to my one and only love, Bob, my husband, editor and lifetime supporter. Thank you for all the light you have brought and continue to bring into my life.

Chapter 1

Melody O'Brien gasped when the sharp knife pressed against the side of her neck. The cold metal sent chills up her spine. From the corner of her eyes, she saw an inmate snap his tattooed, large arm around her throat. The tight grip stung her neck.

She flung both hands on the prisoner, gouging her fingernails into his skin. "Let me go!"

"No way. You're coming with me, bitch. You're mine now." The convict tightened his hold on her. He swung his other arm around Melody's waist, pinching her skin.

Her leg muscles tightened. "Just let me breathe. Please!"

She couldn't tell if her imagination went into overload, or if the guy really loosened his hold on her.

September afternoon sunlight poured through narrow windows near the ceiling in the rotunda of the maximum-security prison in McAlester, Oklahoma.

The prisoner dragged her across the floor. "Run!"

She did as commanded.

The inmate howled in her ear, "Hurry!"

She tried to keep up with her assailant, but she kept tripping every three or four feet. "I'm trying."

"You ain't tryin' hard enough." He pressed the knife more firmly against her neck. "One wrong move and you're dead meat."

The warning wasn't necessary. Melody worked as a prison case manager and knew she needed to surrender to the inmate before he slashed her throat. The sharp metal pressed into her skin. The hairs on the back of her neck rose. Her heart pounded, and sweat popped on her forehead, as she rushed to keep up with the prisoner. She struggled to run faster. Her stomach twisted in knots.

Dozens of shank knives flashed in front of her as inmates fought guards and other prison personnel. Some convicts knocked tables to the floor while others threw food, trays and silverware. Edibles landed and stuck on the walls. Melody attempted to dodge the flying debris, but hot mashed potatoes hit and stung her face. She didn't have time or hands free to wipe the steaming vegetable from her forehead and cheeks, because the inmate kept his stiff grip on her.

She saw some prisoners tearing out wires and equipment in the control room as they cut off communication with the administrative personnel working in the front offices. Inmates swore profusely in the madness. Screams pounded in Melody's ears.

"Keep moving," the prisoner yelled in her ears.

She quickened her pace. Pain pierced through every limb in her body. Fortunately, she wore flats and a pant suit, so she could run fast. She was grateful for her marathon experience. Without the training, she wouldn't have been able to keep up. Apparently, the inmate noticed her running skills.

"I've got to hand it to you. You're in good shape. See, I knew you could do better." He laughed hilariously.

She attempted to turn to identify the guy, but she still couldn't see the man's face. Everything blurred as other prisoners fought with personnel and threw food everywhere.

Then, in the madness, she saw Jordan Lakewater, the man she'd once planned to marry. He raced at a maniac speed down the hall. Dressed in a police uniform, he looked the same as he did three years ago: broad shoulders, black hair and dark eyes. His firm jaw emphasized his part-Cherokee heritage.

She couldn't believe he was here. Sure, she knew she would run into him eventually, since she moved back from Virginia four months ago. The city of McAlester had only 20,000 people. She never expected to see him under such frightening circumstances though.

Inmates scrambled like cockroaches in every direction. Several guards lay on the floor as blood poured from their lifeless bodies. A couple men turned blue.

Just then Jordan passed her, a few feet away. She wanted him to notice her. No such luck. He focused on snapping handcuffs on an inmate. Her heart sank. If only he'd glance her way.

The inmate shoved Melody into a storage room, pushed her forward and then released her. He slammed the door shut. Quickly, at the opportunity, Melody wiped the hot food off her face. She wanted to close her eyes, sigh from relief and take a few deep breaths. She knew from training she needed to keep alert in the dangerous situation.

Melody recognized a couple guards and several other case workers in the room. They looked as terrified as she felt.

The prisoner shoved Melody against the wall and once again placed the side of the knife on her throat. She gave an involuntary moan when she recognized the inmate—Sonny Furemore, leader of the Cobras, the most dangerous gang housed at the prison.

Heart pounding, Melody broke into a sweat. She inhaled sharply to control her breath. She didn't want to let the Cobra leader know she feared him. So did the other prison workers.

She cleared her throat. "Okay, Sonny. What do you want? Just tell us. We'll get you whatever you want."

"She's right," one of the guards spoke up.

"Shut up!" Sonny roared.

Everyone in the room quieted.

With a quick move, Sonny placed the knife in the side of his shoe. "Now, get your lazy bodies behind those boxes and hide. I gotta take good care of my hostages." He laughed outrageously again, showing his gold front tooth.

Melody raced with the other captives to the boxes. Everyone looked like they would break under the strain. They managed to keep quiet. Melody kneeled with them. Then she peeked from the side of the box to see what Sonny would do next.

Just then Jordan burst into the room.

"Jordan!" Melody exclaimed.

Jordan's eyes widened. "Melody! I never expected to see you here. Are you all right?"

Sonny gave a wicked laugh. "Course the bitch's all right. I'm not gonna hurt my hostages, at least not till' I get what I want."

****

In horror, Jordan recognized Sonny as the Cobra gang leader. He helped police capture the convict several years ago during a gang fight which left three people dead and six injured. Sonny grabbed a gun from the inside of his blue prison shirt. Jordan pulled his automatic .40 caliber Glock from his holster and fired twice. Sonny ducked in time to miss one bullet from hitting him directly in the chest, while the second cartridge hit his left leg.

Sonny dropped his weapon, grabbed his bleeding leg and limped to the entrance way. He opened the door, dashed out of the room and into the crowd of wild inmates.

Instead of chasing after him, Jordan let the guy run. It was too dangerous to follow him. Besides, law enforcement flooded the place. Jordan would let them handle Sonny, while he realized his responsibility now included keeping the hostages safe. He needed to help get things under control, and the last person he wanted to see hurt was Melody. What on earth was she doing at a prison anyway? He didn't have time to find the answer. He slammed the door shut and locked it.

Turning, he glanced toward the back of the room as the other hostages slowly rose to their feet. "There're more of you than I thought. Is everyone okay?"

One of the guards nodded. "Yeah, we're good. There's eight of us. What's happening out there?"

Jordan shook his head. "It's a zoo. I've never seen so many shanks in my life. Everyone's trying to kill everyone. You guys, get back down out of sight. I'm assuming none of you have any weapons."

Another guard shook his head. "Right. Thank goodness, you're here. The inmates smashed the control room before we could get to our firearms."

Jordan nodded. "Yeah, several policemen told me. All the local law enforcement units have been called in."

A commotion of yells and screams erupted near the door. Jordan drew his Glock again. "Get behind the boxes to hide. I've got your backs."

The riot victims quickly took cover. Kneeling on one knee, Jordan settled by Melody.

He needed to protect her now. It was the least he could do, considering the part he played in her father's death. He shook his head, attempting to push the terrible event out of his mind. He'd kept the horrible details of the situation from Melody. He planned to keep it that way.

A husky inmate burst through the door. He headed for Jordan.

Still holding the gun, Jordon positioned the weapon at the convict. Perspiration formed on the palms of Jordan's hands as adrenalin rose in his body. He shot, hitting the prisoner in the foot. The convict fell to the floor and pulled a gun from his back pocket. He hit Jordan.

Puffing, Jordan curled in a knot. He landed on the floor. The gun flew from his hand and swirled within inches by Melody. He attempted to get his weapon. Pain shot through his body like sharp mincing arrows he never felt before. Apparently, the bullet scrapped his outer skin and never entered his body. To his surprise, he bled profusely from his nose, and a pool of blood spread on the floor by him. He feared his nose broke, and, from the way his mouth hurt, he actually expected to see several of his teeth scattered across the floor. There were none.

In the madness, he saw Melody grab his Glock and aim at the inmate. The room swirled, and nausea overtook his body. He struggled to keep his eyes open. He couldn't do so. In the darkness, he heard another gunshot. Jordan wondered if Melody shot the inmate. Or did the convict shoot her?

Chapter 2

Melody surprised herself. This was the first time she needed to rely on her shooting training required for the job. Up until now, she feared she would be too afraid to put her skills into action if ever needed.

The inmate fell face down on the floor and didn't move. Another prisoner raced into the room. He madly waved a shank in the air.

Melody's heart pounded and her palms dripped with sweat. She wrapped her forefinger against the trigger again and aimed the weapon at the guy. "Drop your knife!"

Immediately the convict dropped the shank.

"Get your hands up in the air and keep them there." Melody's voice rose.

The inmate shoved his hands upward. He stared at Melody in disbelief and cursed. "What's going on? How did you get that gun?"

Melody wet her dry lips with the tip of her tongue and gave a quick nod. "Get over there in the corner and stay there!"

Keeping his hands high, the inmate scampered to the place.

Feeling a damp hand tap her shoulder, Melody jumped and turned at the same time. Jordan stood. His neck veins protruded, and his body trembled. His brown eyes darted over the room. Then he glanced at her. "It's me. Are you okay?"

Hyperventilating, Melody took a deep breath. "I'm fine now. Are you all right?"

"Yeah, how long was I out?"

"You couldn't have been unconscious for too long. Seconds perhaps. A minute at the most."

"Thanks for taking over. I'll take my gun and cover for you now."

She handed the weapon to him. "Are you ready for this again?"

"Yes." He wiped his hands on his pants and took the firearm.

His hands stopped shaking.

She said, "You look pale."

"I'll be fine. You saved my life."

Melody doubted that.

She never dreamed she would ever work in a prison because of the way her father died in a drug bust three years ago. After she declined Jordan's proposal, she accepted a teaching job in Virginia. Then, when Melody found out Aunt Sharon had a serious heart condition, she moved back to Oklahoma four months ago. Since the McAlester schools didn't have any openings, she was grateful to get the prison job. Now she wondered if taking the position was the biggest mistake she ever made. Even though the penitentiary personnel conducted periodic drills for potential riots, Melody realized the real thing was nothing like the training. Each day at the end of the orientation coaching, she could go home and relax. Would she ever face a calm moment again?

****

Jordon rushed to the door and locked it. He held the man at gunpoint as he contacted Captain Scott via his shoulder radio.

"Yes. What's happening?" Captain Scott avoided the formal hellos.

Jordan cleared his throat. "I need medical assistance in storage room B. I'm holding a prisoner at gunpoint, and another convict is down. The shot inmate is still breathing. He's unconscious though."

"Help is on the way. Is the prisoner giving you any problems?"

"None whatsoever."

"Are you okay?"

"Yes, thank goodness. Melody O'Brien saved my life. She shot an inmate who escaped from us and ran back into the rotunda crowd. After I was shot, she took action. I'd passed out for a couple minutes."

"Where were you hit?"

"The bullet just nicked my arm, and the bleeding has stopped."

"Hang tight. We'll be there shortly."

Jordon backed against a wall. Strange, the captain didn't sound surprised that Melody was at the prison. He wanted to ask Captain Scott if he knew she was there. And why would she be in such a place? There'd be time for those questions later.

Jordan rubbed his sweaty palms on his slacks. "What's the situation where you're at?"

"So far, we've captured six inmates, all Cobras. They were trying to escape the prison grounds."

"So you got all of them."

"Not so fast. The three big gang members are at large. Sonny, Allen and Leo."

His heart pounded. "Oh no! Sonny was here. I should have followed him. I figured it was more important to keep the hostages safe. I should have chased Sonny—"

"Who knows what would have happened if you'd done such a thing? The victims could have been killed."

Jordan wanted to believe the captain. Still he felt guilt. "Do you have any idea where they're headed?"

"Yes, they escaped north through a wooded area back of the prison. A search patrol is out right now. Several other prisoners broke free also. The rest of the inmates are locked up."

"What a nightmare!"

"Yeah, the riot's over from the inside. Now we've got to release the hostages and find the escapees. We're using extra caution all the way. Wait until someone comes to escort all of you out."

Jordan didn't know how much time passed before he heard sirens. Soon three paramedics arrived, and several prison officials entered the room. The medical trio carried the wounded Cobra on a stretcher.

Jordan gave a firm nod to a prison guard. "That guy, whoever he is, needs to be charged with attempted murder."

The guard nodded. "I'll get right on it. Thanks."

After the medics left, Jordan held up his hands and faced the hostages. "Listen, I just spoke with the captain." In minutes, he relayed the information Captain Scott gave him. The hostages, including Melody, grimaced when they heard Sonny, Allen and Leo were at large. Did Melody know about the dangerous trio? He'd ask later.

Jordan placed his hands on his belt. "The good news is the riot's over. We're just waiting now for someone to escort us outside."

Hollers burst forth from everyone.

"Thank goodness, Melody and Jordan were here," one guard exclaimed.

Others joined in similar comments.

One guy turned to Melody. "I'm glad you took control before Jordan came on the scene. You're our heroine."

"Yeah," several men said in unison and high-fived her.

Melody shook her head. "Please, I don't deserve all this credit you're giving me. I don't know what I would have done without Lieutenant Lakewater. I was terrified."

Tears in her eyes, she turned to Jordan. "How can I ever thank you?"

A slow grin spread across Jordan's face. "I can't believe you asked me. You saved my life! Remember?"

"I highly doubt it."

"I don't, not for one minute," Jordan wanted her to know.

He gave her a hug. Smelling Melody's rose-scented perfume, Jordan remembered how he'd loved the woman and how excited they were about a possible future together. Her father, McAlester's police chief, introduced her to him, and two years later, Jordan proposed. At the time, Melody said she could never be a policeman's wife. She said it would be too emotionally painful, knowing her husband would be facing potential danger on a daily basis. He considered leaving the police force then and getting a different job for her sake. Law enforcement was in his blood though. So Melody headed to Virginia to teach high school English where she planned to stay. What happened? Why was she in

McAlester now? And, in a prison, of all places? Was she visiting someone perhaps?

"Yeah, Melody. You need to give yourself credit too," one of the guards said. "Remember, we didn't have any weapons to protect us."

Jordan nodded and slowly released Melody. "I agree. Everyone, come with me. Let's get out of here." He held his hand for Melody.

She took it.

Inside, he wanted to melt. He forgot how soft her hand always felt to his touch.

He looked her way. "Just why did you happen to be in McAlester? Especially at the prison?"

She sighed. "I work there as a case manager."

Jordan frowned.

She nodded. "It's a long story. I'm living here with my aunt now."

"And you didn't bother to at least call?"

She raised her eyebrows. "I'll explain later. I'm still shaken from everything."

He gave her hand a quick squeeze. "Sorry, I understand. It's great to see you again."

She looked at him and gave him a smile which melted his heart. "Nice to see you too."

For the first time, Jordan noted what Melody wore, a green pant suit with a yellow and green scarf. Green earrings gleamed on her tiny ear lobes and her long, red hair sparkled in the sunshine.

How could he have let this woman leave several years ago? He still didn't know. Yet, what was he supposed to do? She'd turned down his proposal. Period.

Outside, people rushed down the prison steps. In the distance, cameras flashed from the media, surrounded by a group of people. Jordan released his hand from Melody. Everyone embraced everyone and told them of their love for each other. Thrilled at the outcome, Jordan watched people return to safety.

When Jordan saw Captain Scott, the two gave each other a bear hug. Then Jordan placed his hand gently across Melody's back with his fingers spread. Her warmth penetrated his hand. He needed to touch her again, to know she really was safe. For now anyway. He hated to think of the aftermath about to take place. Who knew what would happen? He never felt comfortable until an investigation was over, and this one was just beginning. If anything else happened to his dear Melody…He stopped. She wasn't his. Not anymore. She already made that clear long ago. Quickly, he returned his focus to the present.

Captain Scott grinned at Melody. "I'm thrilled to see you're okay. If you hadn't shot Tim Barlow, we'd be in more trouble than we're already in. He was one of the most dangerous prison gang leaders, who originally came from California. Right now, we're looking especially for three other big Cobras."

Melody shook her head. "I just didn't know what to do. I'm quite nauseated from everything."

"Quite normal under the circumstances. You did the right thing," Captain Scott echoed the words Jordan said earlier.

Melody crossed her arms. "Does anyone know yet if the shot was fatal?"

Jordan noticed the quiver in her voice.

Captain Scott shook his head. "We don't know yet. He just left on the ambulance."

"Don't worry," Jordan suggested. "You did what

you needed to do, regardless of his outcome."

Captain Scott nodded. "Amen." He glanced back at Jordan. "How are you?"

Melody frowned. "He lost a lot of blood."

The captain drew his eyebrows together. "You need to go to the hospital. I'll take you."

Jordan fought a tingling sensation in his stomach. "I'm fine."

"Captain Scott's right. You look terrible." Melody pursued her lips.

Grinning, Jordan looked at her. "Thanks for the compliment."

She flung her hands to her mouth. "I didn't mean it the way it sounded." A dimple dotted her check. "I'm sorry."

Jordan waved his hand. "No apology needed."

The captain looked Jordan's way. "I agree with Melody. Let's get you to the emergency room to have the doctor take a look at your injuries."

He didn't say anything further. He dreaded going to ER. The last time he was there, he was with Melody's dying father. He didn't want to relive the past. Jordan remembered how close Melody was with her dad, probably because her mother died at a young age from breast cancer. Her father's death was difficult for Jordan too. Her father treated him like a son. Jordan felt if…if only he had saved her father! After Mr. O'Brien died, Melody asked for details about his death, but Jordon didn't plan to tell anyone his secret.

Especially Melody.

Chapter 3

Outside, the media spread through the crowd as they asked questions. If the news reporters found out Melody had shot a man, they'd want to talk to her. The last thing she wanted was people asking her to relive what just happened. She needed to get home to Aunt Sharon, her dear second mother. Her aunt probably heard of the riot by this time. She watched a couple game shows every day, and the prison disturbance no doubt made national television. Her aunt would be worried sick if she heard about the event.

She looked at the captain. "Could you do me a favor?"

Captain Scott nodded. "Name it."

"Can you get me away from the media and home to Aunt Sharon? If she heard the news, she's terrified. I carpooled today with my best friend, Kim Winters. I don't see her around here anywhere. I'm worried about her too."

Captain Scott glanced at the crowd. "Don't worry about Kim. She's probably somewhere here, and I agree. If the media finds you, they'll bombard you with questions. Sure, I can take you home. It's the least I can do. Follow me as though you aren't with me."

Melody got behind the captain. "Sounds good." She turned to Jordan. The two of them stood so close she could see tiny, black specks in his dark brown eyes. "You better get to the hospital quick. I'll check on you later."

He shook his head. "I'm fine."

Melody's heart fell. Did he mean he didn't want to see her again? She hoped not.

He put his arm gently on her back. "I'm coming with you."

"Then we're going to the hospital first. I can call Aunt Sharon from my cell phone when we get in the car."

"Great idea." The captain nodded.

Jordan grinned. "Wait a minute. Don't I have anything to say about this?"

"No," Melody and Captain Scott said in unison.

Melody looked at him. "Actually, you don't have a choice on this one." She placed her hand in the curve of his right arm, as his injured arm hung limply at his side. Mercy. She forgot how her arm fit just right in the crook of his, as though they belonged together.

Quickly, the three wormed through the crowd with Melody and Jordan following the captain. When they reached the police vehicle, Jordan opened a door for her.

They stood so near she smelled his spicy scent. Oh, it felt good to see him again. She squelched her feelings. No way could she allow her heart to reignite for a guy she could never have. She wasn't a fool; she knew things were too late for her and Jordan.

She climbed into the back seat. "I should be opening the door for you. I want you to take care of your arm."

"I didn't use my injured arm."

She wanted to argue, but she couldn't. For the first time, she noticed he did use his good arm. She should have seen what was happening around her. Her face reddened. Why was she acting like some high school girl? It was like she couldn't think if the man stood close to her.

"Are you okay?" she asked. "You're getting awfully pale."

"I'll be okay, thanks."

After everyone got in the car, they snapped on seat belts. Captain Scott eased the vehicle onto a back road of the prison.

Turning, Melody glanced out the window. She noted luscious green oak and maple trees passed by as they drove. Fluffy clouds scattered across the sky. *How could something so bad happen on such a pretty day?* She looked back at the crowd. Obviously, no one from the media saw them, because no one was following them.

"Captain Scott, you're a genius. We dodged the media. Thanks a million. I just didn't want to face them. Or anyone else, except Kim and my aunt."

Turning, Jordan grinned at Melody. "I don't blame you. It's like Captain Scott said though. Kim's no doubt fine. I wouldn't worry about her. You've got enough to deal with right now."

For a moment, Melody wondered if Jordan changed. It wasn't like him not to voice concern over something like not being able to see Kim. She was a case manager too. Yet, the captain told her the same thing. Wasn't the law enforcement worried about her good friend? The moment she asked the question, she stopped herself. Jordan was right. She fretted too much over Kim. First, Jordan needed to get to the hospital; then she needed to check on her aunt. Then, she could find Kim's whereabouts. Besides, if anything terrible happened to her friend, surely she would have heard about it. Bad news traveled fast.

Interrupting her thoughts, a black sedan with dark

tinted windows whisked by as several guys swung their heads in the fresh air and shot at the police car.

"Hold on!" Captain Scott snapped on the siren and started a high speed chase. "I'm breaking the rules with Melody in the back seat. Sometimes rules have to be broken."

"I couldn't agree more." Jordan reached for his gun. "Melody, get down. You'll have to take off your seat belt."

Melody surprised herself at how fast she reacted. In seconds, she snapped off the strap and dashed onto the car floor. Both Captain Scott and Jordan pulled their guns and aimed out the window. Shots burst like cannon fire and rang out, obliterating the neighborhood into fear.

At the sound of bullets hitting the car, Melody's heart jumped. Up to this point, the shots missed her. How long could this go on? And what about Jordan? Was he all right? Apparently Captain Scott still controlled the car. Melody didn't know how fast they were going. She'd never been in a vehicle at such roller-coaster speed before. Her stomach churned at the motion. Her long fingernails dug into the floor mats. Her palms were damp from perspiration, and her knees trembled.

Suddenly, she felt a sharp jolt. They'd obviously turned onto a gravel road. The car bounced every way imaginable. Several seconds later, the vehicle came to a screeching halt. Still on the floor, she heard Captain Scott snap off the engine.

"Stay on the floor," the captain instructed.

"Right." She needed to restrain herself from automatically getting up to see what was happening.

She couldn't afford to raise her head and resume her seat though, not now, not yet. Her life was at stake. She remained on the floor. The next thing she heard was Jordan and Captain Scott pop their doors open.

Shouts of protest, including strings of profanity, from several guys, rang into the still air. Several moments later, Melody heard her car door in the back snap open. Beads of perspiration formed on her forehead. Who was there? Jordan? Captain Scott? A Cobra? After what happened so far, she couldn't be sure. She squeezed her eyes tight and hoped for the best.

"Melody," Jordan said.

Her eyes flung open and her head popped up at the same time.

"Thank goodness, it's you. I was so afraid."

"You're doing great. It's safe to get up. We got the bad guys arrested. Are you okay?"

"Yes, I'm fine."

Relief flooded over her, and she welcomed the fact she was out of harm's way, at least for the moment.

****

Puffing from being out of breath, Jordan nodded, and his heart went out to Melody. Hadn't she been through enough for one day? Certainly this day was far from typical for the woman he once loved.

He held his hand out to her with his uninjured arm. "Here, let me help you out of the car."

She accepted his support. He welcomed the warmth of Melody's hand. Why was he feeling this way? Surely, he was only doing his best to protect her. He didn't still have feelings for her. Did he? Abruptly, he stopped his insane thoughts. He couldn't afford to think this way. He wanted to be rational and protect Melody.

He also needed to seek medical attention. He was glad Melody and Captain Scott were so persistent about

Mary Ann Kerl

getting him to the doctor. His nose and left arm ached beyond belief. An X-ray or two would give him reassurance, which was something he desperately needed right now. Also, with Melody by his side, things wouldn't seem so bad. *Stop it! Stop thinking this way*, he warned himself. *Melody left you. Remember?*

The touch of her feminine soft skin warmed his heart. Even though he continued using his right arm, pain kept piercing his wounded left arm. He helped Melody get off her knees and onto the seat. Automatically, he reached over to help with her seat belt. His neck hair rose from their nearness. He scowled at himself for acting this way. Their relationship was over. So, why was his body reacting like this? As hard as it was, Jordan forced himself to leave Melody in the back seat. He closed her door, got in front and fastened his seat belt.

"Ready?" Captain Scott was already in his seat.

"As ready as I'll ever be." He slammed his door shut.

Pain raced through him, and a flashback of the emotional turmoil he'd suffered after Melody's father's death came to his mind. Melody decided then they couldn't be together... Now he faced those aching memories again. He didn't know which distress was more exhausting: the physical or the emotional. A throbbing shot through his nostrils. His ribs hurt too. So did every bone in his body. For the first time, since the riot, he noted and admitted he was terrified. *What am I scared of? A million things!* He gave a heavy sigh. For one thing, the agony seemed more than he could bear. Just how bad were his injuries? For another thing, he couldn't afford to take off work. The investigation was top priority on the police agenda.

He worried about Melody too. Sure, she'd been the epitome of bravery this afternoon, but what about when she returned home? And why did she work at the prison now, a place in the past she feared? A million questions he had for her exploded in his mind. This wasn't the time or place to ask them.

Briefly, he shook his head as though it would clear his thoughts. It didn't.

Exactly how would Melody handle the riot aftermath? He knew from experience the emotional turmoil of shooting a man was hard to deal with. Yet, he firmly believed everyone had a right to defend themselves. Every person needed protection in the face of danger, and law enforcement work gave him a chance to help people be safe, which was more rewarding than he could say. Why did someone like Melody have to go through something like this? She was such a lovely woman.

Bang! Bang! Bang!

Jordan's heart pounded. Turning as far as possible in his seat, he could hardly believe what he saw, yet he knew this wasn't a dream. Another black sedan passed by. Several other guys popped their heads out of the windows and shot at the police car again. Obviously, more inmates escaped from the prison than officials first thought.

"Oh no!" Melody screamed.

"Get down again!" Jordan reached for his Glock.

"Yes!" Captain Scott agreed. "I'm afraid we're not going to the hospital just yet."

Melody snapped off her seat belt and flung back on the floor.

Chapter 4

Melody's heart pounded. *When will this nightmare ever end?* Her nails turned white. She gripped her fingers deeper into the car mat. A loud shot banged against the window above her.

Now what was happening? Were these gunmen ahead of them?

Bang! Another shot blasted. With a loud screech, the car swung into a sharp turn and stopped.

She heard Jordan say, "Let me get him."

Holding still, she listened carefully. Apparently, Jordan had opened his car door and stepped outside. He slammed the door shut.

"What's happening?" Melody whispered to the captain.

"Hang tight," the officer mumbled softly. "Don't let anyone see you."

"Okay."

A couple more shots rang.

"I've gotta get out. Stay down," he whispered to Melody.

"I will." Melody held her breath.

The door banged shut. Then the angry voices came.

"Hands up!" Captain Scott yelled from outside.

Seconds later, her car door snapped open.

"Jordan!" She sighed with relief. When she glanced up, she saw a man with a black mask over his head.

Her heart began beating rapidly. Melody recognized a Cobra sign on his hand, a coiled snake. The gang member yanked her out of the car so fast, she got dizzy. Before she knew what was happening, the guy threw her down in the back seat of another vehicle, a white Corolla. He got in the back and stepped on her head with his boot.

"Stay down!" he hissed, taking his foot off her. He slapped an arm against the front seat. "Give 'er the gun. Let's get outta' here."

The driver took off at high speed. Melody felt like she was going to throw up. She tried to lift her head.

"Stay down," the man in back hissed.

Moments passed, with the car yanking from one lane to another. The vehicle turned and hit several potholes as they combed over rough terrain. Melody no longer heard traffic.

"You can get up now, sweetie. This is gonna be one wild ride. Better fasten your seat belt."

Unlike Jordan's caring help earlier, this guy wasn't about to help Melody to her seat. She placed her hands on the leather upholstery and raised her body to a sitting position. She glanced back to see if Jordan and Captain Scott were in sight. She couldn't see them anywhere. All she could make out were clouds of road dust. She didn't even recognize the territory.

"Uh uh, baby doll," the man by her snarled. With his large hand, he turned her head. "Don't look back. You ain't seen nothin.' Ya' hear."

"Yes," Melody responded. She wasn't about to argue with the Cobra. Besides, she didn't see anything, except for dirt. Turning, she noted the driver also wore a mask. Who were the men anyway? Did she know them?

Melody's cell phone rang. She jumped.

"Don't answer it." The guy in back pulled off his mask.

Melody panted. It was Sonny. How could she get away from him before he killed her? Her facial muscles pulled into a tightness, and her forehead pounded the beginning of a migraine.

The driver removed his disguise also. Melody recognized him too: Allen McDonald. She wondered what happened to the third outlaw: Leo Shiver. The trio was well-known big time by prison officials.

The phone kept ringing.

"Give it to me!" Sonny snapped at her.

Melody retrieved the cell from her pocket. She refused to hand it over. She didn't want the criminals to get any information, like her contacts. A sudden idea came to her. The concept was risky. She needed to be brave and try every possible outlet though. Fortunately, the window was open. Swinging her arm, she threw the phone out the window. It bounced across prairie land and disappeared into tall grass. Perhaps someone would find the cell and rescue her, Melody thought.

Sonny hissed through his teeth. "You gonna play smart, huh?"

Melody said nothing.

"Stop this car. Get the phone," Sonny ordered.

Allen turned the steering wheel sharp. The car went airborne, flying over a ditch, and landed in a pasture. Allen kept driving, hitting potholes and bumps.

Leaning forward, Sonny slammed his fists on the front seat. "Quite hitting these bumps. Stop the car!"

Allen jerked his head back and glared at Sonny. His eye's bulged and his nostrils flared. "I'm tryin.' You don't want me to roll the car, do ya?" He turned back towards the front.

A couple of seconds later, Allen stopped the Corolla with a jolt, sending Melody against the door. Her arm took a bad hit.

Allen opened his door and raced out the car.

Sonny remained in the vehicle. "You dummy! She threw the phone over there." He pointed.

Turning on one foot, Allen stopped running and faced Sonny. "How do ya' expect me to know? She was in the backseat and I was in the front. I need help."

Sonny groaned. "You're a sorry sight." He opened his door, got out and gave Melody a cold stare. "I'm gonna find the phone, come hell or high water."

He took off limping in the field.

Melody thought this was her chance to make a getaway. Some bushes were behind her, on the other side of the road. She waited a moment until Sonny's back was toward her. She sneaked out the vehicle, leaving the car door open. She raced ahead, in the opposite direction.

The bushes were a few feet from the car, and, in no time, Melody got to them. She started shuffling to the middle of the greenery. She stopped. Turning, she peeked from a couple of long, broken, tree branches, covered with leaves, to see Sonny and Allen's whereabouts. The two ran in different directions like mad men. Apparently, they didn't see her. Yet.

Melody searched for a secure area to hide. She knew the moment they discovered her missing, they'd start looking for her. She headed farther into the shrubs. Her brain was in high gear, thinking of an escape route. She detected a fish odor. She must be near Lake Eufaula.

"Hey, hold it!" Sonny shouted. "The bitch's outta the car. We've gotta find her."

Sonny hobbled with his injured leg as he headed her direction. She raced farther ahead again. Twigs snapped and scratched her arms. A deserted beach area near the lake wasn't far from her. Still running, she quickly looked behind her. Sonny got closer. He apparently didn't spot her. He looked from one side to the other as he kept struggling.

She ran for the water. Since the beach was tiny, it didn't take long to get to the lake. She took a deep breath and submerged her body in the cold liquid. She hoped she wouldn't have to hold her breath too long. Under water, she heard Sonny and Allen approaching.

Sonny yelled, "She disappeared. How? She's bound to be somewhere near here."

Still under water, Melody kept holding her breath. The cold water pierced every cell in her body. She heard the men talk as they ran off. She couldn't make out what they were saying. She longed to come up for air. Now! When her face came to the surface, she started puffing. Sonny and Allen ran with their backs to her.

Giving the area another scan, Melody realized it was no use to try to swim across the lake. Impossible.

Suddenly, she got an idea: go to the bushes and climb the tall cottonwood tree to her right. If she got high enough, maybe she could hide under the branches and leaves. She raced there. She wrapped her legs around the trunk as far as possible and began crawling upward. Twigs broke and branches slapped in her face. The wind picked up. She scraped her ankles on the bark. About halfway up, every leg muscle began to hurt. She wouldn't give up. She tried to overcome the pain by forcing her body to the limit, until she reached the higher branches to hide. She kept climbing upward.

When Melody reached the first tree branch, she needed to catch her breath. She didn't rest long, however. Not enough time. Even though Sonny and Allen kept dashing away from her, she could hear their voices. When she got a couple branches higher, she sprawled on a huge limb and under the tree leaves. Straining to listen, she watched them carefully through the foliage.

Instead of running, they now walked. Apparently, they were tired too. As they turned toward her, she held her breath.

Sonny leaned on the vehicle as he grabbed his leg. "I'm bleeding' again. Ya' gotta help me. Quick!"

Melody watched Allen open a car door and retrieve a bag. She kept viewing as he pulled something from the sack.

He shouted to Sonny. "Hold still. I got a pair of eye tweezers." He raced back to Sonny.

"Do you think you can get it out?"

"Yeah, I see the bullet. It's just under the skin."

Sonny swore. "Hurry, it hurts!"

"How do I remove it, bro, when you're flying all over the place?"

Sonny gritted his teeth and hissed, "Thanks for the support, you egg head."

A moment later, Melody saw Allen hold the bullet high in the air with his tweezers. "I got it."

"Sew me up," Sonny roared.

"Hey, I ain't no doc," Allen snapped.

Sonny pointed. "Wrap the rag around my leg. Maybe that'll stop the bleeding, and get me the bottle of liquor from the bag."

Seconds later, Allen held the flask in front of Sonny, who took several long gulps of the alcohol.

Allen shook his head. "Better go easy on the liquid there. I don't want to have to go back to steal more."

"You may have to, dude. I'm in Painesville."

Allen looked at Sonny's leg. "The bleeding's slowing down."

"Keep an eye on it."

A moment later, Allen slowly untied the towel. "Hey, I'm a pretty good doc, even if I do say so myself. The bleedin' stopped. I think all we need now are some bandages."

Sonny guzzled a couple more drinks of whiskey. "I'm feeling better by the minute too. Soon as I get a little more of this stuff in me, we'll hunt down the lady, then take off in the woods and head for my cousin's place in Tulsa."

Allen flashed a wicked grin. "Will we be able to hide there?"

Sonny wiped his mouth with the back of his blue, prison, shirt sleeve. "Trust me. He's done it for me before."

Allen snickered. "Sounds like a good relative to me."

Sirens wailed as the emergency vehicles approached. Her heart beat wildly. Could it be possible she would be able to make an escape after all?

Sonny limped to his feet. "Get to the car. It's the fuzz. Help me."

Melody watched Allen assist Sonny to the vehicle. In seconds, they got in the Corella and drove over the rugged territory, leaving piles of dust behind. They raced up a hill and out of sight. Even though she couldn't see any other vehicles, she heard the sirens get louder.

With Sonny and Allen gone, she began climbing

down the tree. If she hurried, she could get to the highway and flag one of the police cars down. She expected to see them merge from the high hill any second. Inside, she felt excitement and hope grow.

Then something crawled onto her leg. She looked down to see a rattle snake. She broke into a sweat. What if the snake bit her? Would she even be able to make it down the tree?

As the snake slithered across her leg, chills sprawled up her back. She didn't move, knowing how important it was not to panic. Slowly, the rattler crawled farther up her body. Melody lay still. The snake slithered off her upper body and up the branch. Her lips parted, and she let out a deep breath of relief. After the snake was out of sight, she scrambled down the tree.

****

Meanwhile, Captain Scott dropped Jordan off the emergency room of McAlester Regional about thirty minutes earlier.

Captain Scott placed a hand on Jordan's shoulder. "I'll leave you here, and I'll join the police search for Melody, if you'll be okay."

"I'll be fine. I wish I could help you."

"Don't worry. We've got tons of men looking for her already. You need to get your arm taken care of. I think it's more important I join the search."

Jordon nodded. "I'm afraid I can't argue."

In the hospital, bright, florescent, lights glared.

Jordan smelled an antiseptic odor as two orderlies helped him into the emergency room. An elderly man, wearing a white jacket, entered.

"Jordan, what're you doing here?"

The two men'd known each other, since Jordan was

a child.

"Hi Dr. Thompson. A bullet just scraped my arm."

"Looks like more than a scrape. Please, get on the table, and I'll take a look. It's great to see you again. I wish the circumstances were better. We heard about the riot on TV."

Jordan settled on the long table. "Yeah, I'm just glad it's over."

Fifteen minutes later, after an examination, Dr. Thompson nodded. "You're going to need some X-rays. Prepare yourself. You may have broken your nose." The doctor hesitated and patted Jordan's shoulder. "And perhaps a rib or two. We'll find out."

"Whatever you say, Doc."

Back in the waiting room, Jordan sighed deeply as he took a seat. He positioned his injured left arm on the edge of the orange hospital chair. He wasn't comfortable. So he placed his right hand gently in the curve of his left arm to give it a steady hold. However, the pain escalated. His right hand involuntarily flung back as though he'd touched a hot stove. Shifting from one side of the chair to the other, Jordan refrained from picking up a magazine. He couldn't concentrate now, too much on his mind, not to mention the physical discomfort.

The receptionist asked him, "Would you care for something to drink while you wait for the doctor?"

"I'd love something like a soda pop. Where's the vending machine?"

"Just down the hallway and to your left."

"Thanks." He stood and headed for the doorway.

Clumsily, he marched to the red vending apparatus and reached in his pocket for change. Seconds later, back in his seat, the carbonated beverage soothed his dry throat. At least the drink offered a little comfort to him in the midst of his suffering. He glanced down at his uniform. Dried blood partially covered his shirt, from his earlier nose bleeding.

The doctor came into the waiting room and motioned to him. "Come on, and step back into my office. I've got the X-rays."

"Great." Jordan took the last sip of his soda and dropped the can in a nearby waste paper basket.

In the doctor's office, Jordan took a seat. The doctor settled behind a large desk. Several large plants set in a couple corners, surrounding a bookshelf, which reached from the floor to the ceiling.

The doctor nodded. "It was a bad fall. Even so, and don't ask me how this happened, you don't have any broken bones. Of course, you bruised the hell out of your internal organs. You also sprained your left wrist. I know you've got to be in agony. Don't worry. I'm prescribing some pain medication for you."

"Thanks, not necessary though. I can handle everything on my own."

Slowly, Dr. Thompson raised his eyebrows and grinned. "And when did you morph from a policeman into a doctor?"

"No offense, but I know pain medicine makes a person groggy, and I've got to have a clear head for this investigation."

"Trust me. You'll need some medication for the evening. You'll also need to get a lot of rest for a week or two. I want you to cut your work hours some. I don't want you to overdue. Even if no bones broke, you still need time for the healing necessary to take place internally."

Jordan sighed. Everything was happening fast. He wondered about his team, if the gang members were still at large. He hoped not. But he feared the police probably wouldn't get so lucky to find the escapees so soon.

The doctor rose from his seat and patted Jordan's shoulder. "I know it's hard. Give it time. Eventually, you'll feel better."

"I need to keep working for the investigation. Three dangerous prisoners are at large, plus several others. We need to capture them as soon as possible."

The doctor shook his head. "Yes, I heard the news on television. I realize you have to work. Make sure to rest too. Okay?"

Jordan nodded. "Fair enough, Doc."

Leaving the doctor's office, Jordan scanned the hallway for Captain Scott. Apparently he wasn't back yet. He hoped Melody was home safe by now. With Aunt Sharon.

From out of nowhere, a man jumped from a room and walked by Jordan. It was Leo Shiver.

He snickered. "Just walk like nothing is happening."

Heart pounding, Jordan lifted his chin and gave Leo a curt nod as he kept walking. He attempted to reach for his gun without the inmate seeing him.

Leo raised his eyebrows. "And, if you get out your gun, your friend Melody will be shot."

Jordan jerked his head. "What do you mean?"

"Exactly what I said. You've got brains. Figure it out."

"What do you want?" Jordan attempted to speak calmly. Then, before Leo could answer, Jordan yelled, "Help!" and grabbed Leo in a head hold. Pain raced through his body. Both fell to the floor.

Several people, including a couple security guards, raced down the hall and grabbed Leo from Jordan. Puffing, Jordan pulled out his handcuffs and arrested Leo.

One of the security guards looked at Jordan. "Looks like you're bleeding. We'll take it from here." He nodded to the other guard. "See if the doctor can see him again right away."

The security man nodded. "Sure thing." He fled down the hall.

Jordan let the guard pull him back to his feet as Leo stood in handcuffs. Jordan looked at him. "You're being wise not to try to run away."

Leo's nostrils flared. "Whatever."

"Now, where are Sonny and Allen?"

Leo snickered. "I don't snitch on my friends."

Two other hospital security officers arrived on the scene. One looked at Jordan. "Don't worry. We've contacted the prison and told them to come pick up their man."

Jordan nodded. "Good. Could you please tell the warden that Leo needs to be taken in for some serious interrogation?"

"Of course," one of the security men said.

Leo gave a mocking laugh and looked at Jordan. "Good luck with that. Like I said, I don't snitch on my friends."

Chapter 5

Back at the lake, sirens blasted. Still in wet clothes, Melody shivered. The police car alarms got louder. Melody climbed down the tree and raced toward the highway, through the brush and onto pasture land. Three cars appeared. She jumped up and down, hoping one of the policemen would see her. From being the daughter of a law enforcement officer, Melody knew when more than one police car arrived on a scene, the emergency was serious.

One police cruiser swept by as she frantically pranced while running up a deep ditch, closer to the road. The second car went by as fast as the first one. She nearly lost hope when the third car screeched to a stop.

It was Captain Scott. He got out of the car. "Are you all right?"

Weakly, she nodded. "I think so. Have you found Aunt Sharon?"

"Not yet. We've been calling and have several policemen looking for her." He opened his car trunk and handed her a clean, thick towel. "You can use this to dry off."

"Thanks." She took the item and dried her arms, legs and face. "How's Jordan?"

"I didn't have a chance to pick him up yet. The doctor said he'd be checking him thoroughly and giving him X-rays."

She frowned. "Can we get him now?"

"First, let's get you to Aunt Sharon's to change clothes. I'm sure you're freezing, and perhaps your aunt is home by now. Maybe she's napping."

Melody nodded. "Maybe. She wears a C-pap and has a hard time hearing the phone when it's on."

"We'll find her."

She smiled at the captain. "Thanks. After I get into some dry clothes, can we get Jordan?"

"Sure. Can you tell me what transpired so far?" He helped her to the car.

Inside the vehicle, she told him about what she saw and overheard with Sonny and Allen. Using his phone, the captain quickly relayed Melody's information to various police and prison sources.

Moments later, they approached the McAlester city limits.

Melody looked at Captain Scott. "How was I so lucky to have stumbled onto you on the highway?"

"We formed a team to search for you. People from all over the community came to volunteer."

"Oh my." Tears came to her eyes at the realization others were looking out for her and caring for her safety. "We better inform them you found me."

"I already radioed the information when I saw you by the road. We're keeping the rescue team out to keep looking for Sonny and Allen."

Melody glanced at Captain Scott. "You guys are on the ball."

He grinned. "Your father would appreciate the remark."

Melody chuckled. "Yeah."

Leaning back on the seat, Melody felt like she

needed a moment to catch her breath.

The captain glanced her way. "Please realize that we're doing everything we can to find your aunt."

Nervously, Melody bit a fingernail. "I know. I'm so worried. She has a heart condition, you know."

"Yes, we know."

"What about Kim? Did you find her?"

Melody didn't know if it was her imagination, or if Captain Scott's face flushed.

He gave a nervous cough. "Don't worry. We'll get in touch with her."

How could he be so sure? She wanted to ask, but she didn't feel like now was the time. She knew Captain Scott had enough on his mind. Still, it wasn't like him not to be more concerned about Kim.

Moments later, the captain pulled his police car in front of Aunt Sharon's home. Melody glanced at the old, Victorian house. Painted mint green, the building featured white trimmed windows and shutters. A big magnolia tree graced the front yard. Rows of marigolds and petunias were by the large front porch, which featured a wooden swing for two people.

The captain tilted his head and looked at Melody. "I'll go with you inside. Be careful. We don't know what we may be dealing with."

"Of course." Melody nodded in understanding, retrieving her house key from her purse.

She dashed up the steps with Captain Scott. She tried to open the door. It wasn't locked. Aunt Sharon always locked the front door. Frowning, she turned to the captain and shrugged. The policeman nodded to Melody in understanding. He put a finger to his lips and pulled his gun.

She crept in the entryway with the captain and picked up the mail, dropped via the door slot. On top of the ads, Melody spotted a handwritten envelope addressed to her. There was no stamp. Odd. After Captain Scott checked her house, she would open the strange letter with no official post date. With the policeman by her side, she dashed into the living room and set the postal deliveries on the walnut coffee table.

In the corner, the grandfather clock struck three o'clock. When they entered Aunt Sharon's bedroom, Melody's stomach gripped in fear. Scattered on the floor were bed sheets and a red, flowered comforter. Melody knew her aunt, an immaculate housekeeper, would never leave her bedroom in such a manner. A jewelry box, open and empty, set on the floor. One of the windows was partially up, and the screen was missing.

"Oh no!" Melody said.

"Shhh, follow me," the captain whispered.

Melody nodded and kept quiet. Captain Scott had his gun aimed and ready. The situation looked like a television movie, but Melody knew everything was real. She followed him until they covered every room. Aunt Sharon wasn't in sight.

The captain put his gun back in the holster. "Looks like it's safe for you to change clothes now. I'll wait in the living room. Try not to disturb the crime scene. I'm calling for an investigation. My officers will be here shortly."

"Right." Melody bit her lip and pinched her throat as she darted to her bedroom. There, she grabbed dry clothes and slipped into them in record time. Several moments later and fully dressed, Melody went back to Captain Scott in the living room.

He nodded. "My officers are on the way."

"Good."

When they arrived, the policemen set up equipment to take fingerprints. Melody moved nervously in the room. Where was Aunt Sharon anyway?

She picked up the letter from the table. "I got this in the mail. It has no stamp."

The captain cleared his throat. "Yes, I noticed."

Melody raised her eyebrows. "You did?"

"Couldn't help it, sticks out like a sore thumb. I think you should open it now. Please realize, I'm not trying to be nosy."

Melody shook her head. "Of course. I want you with me just in case it's something bad."

"Good idea." Captain Scott pulled out a pair of plastic gloves and handed them to her.

"Thanks." Still shaking from the day's events, Melody put on the gloves and carefully opened the letter to avoid tearing anything.

The note said: *Welcome to our jungle. You're next.*

She took several deep breaths to calm herself and handed the note to the captain.

He put on another set of plastic gloves, took the message, read it and shook his head. "I don't want to scare you, but it doesn't look good. The Cobras may have found out you shot one of their own. I'm having the men check this for fingerprints."

Captain Scott carefully placed the note in a plastic bag and removed his gloves. With drooped shoulders, Melody stripped her hands free of the plastic coverings.

She sighed. Did the note come from a Cobra?

Captain Scott gave the plastic sack, holding the message, to one of the other policeman. "You need to check this for fingerprints. It's a note Miss O'Brien received. It came with the mail and didn't have a stamp on it." He looked at Melody. "Come on. Let's you and I do a little searching for your aunt also. You can take me to some of the homes in your neighborhood to see if anyone saw or heard something."

"Great idea. Now, what about Jordan?"

"He'll wait for us."

Captain Scott escorted Melody back outside. She took a deep breath of fresh air as an attempt to calm herself. It didn't work. She'd never been in such potential danger before.

Melody looked at the captain. "Shall we go to Hendrick's home first? They live a block from here and my aunt visits them a lot, nearly every day."

Captain Scott grinned. "You're beginning to think like a cop. Let's go. I know them too."

Moments later, Captain Scott and Melody stood on the porch of the home. The captain pressed the doorbell.

In seconds, Mrs. Hendrick answered. "Melody! Are you okay? I heard the news, and I didn't want to come over while the police were there."

"I'm fine."

"Come in!" The gray-haired woman motioned with her hands.

Inside, she hugged Melody so hard that Melody actually felt her body hurt.

"Do you have any idea where Aunt Sharon might be?"

Quickly, Mrs. Hendrick backed from the embrace. "No, I don't."

Captain Scott looked at the older lady. "We thought she could be here. Would your husband know where she could be?"

Mrs. Hendrick rubbed her hands on her blue paisley dress. "Oh no!"

"What's wrong?" Melody knew Mrs. Hendrick well. She could see the kind woman became extremely upset after Captain Scott asked to see her husband.

"I was going to ask Melody if she'd seen him."

The captain raised his dark eyebrows. "He's not home?"

"No, I went to the grocery store a little while ago, and when I got back, he was gone. He didn't leave a note or anything."

"Oh?" Captain Scott inquired. "Is that unusual?"

Mrs. Hendrick nodded. "Very. Not once in our fifty-two years of marriage has he ever forgot to leave me a note."

Captain Scott pinched his chin with two fingers. "Do you have voice mail?"

"Yes. I've already checked for messages though. The only one I got was from a salesperson."

"How about texting?"

"I've already checked my cell for any texts too. I'll check again." Mrs. Hendrick went to the I-phone on a nearby end table. She punched a couple of numbers and shook her head. "Nothing." She took a deep breath, making her shoulders rise. "I'm getting more worried. I need to show the two of you something. Come with me."

Melody and Captain Scott followed Mrs. Hendrick down the yellow, carpeted hallway and into her husband's office, lined with windows on the west wall. Early afternoon sunlight burst through, giving a golden glow to the room.

Mrs. Hendrick shuffled to a desk and picked up a

sheet of paper. "Here's another unusual thing about my husband."

She handed the paper to Captain Scott. He took it and started reading. Seconds later, he shrugged. "It looks like your husband was working on one of his novels. What's so unusual about an author engaging in that activity?"

Mrs. Hendrick swirled to the captain and pointed to a spot in the writing. "He stopped in the middle of a sentence."

"So?" Melody asked.

"My husband never writes in such a manner. He does his research and then completes ten pages in one setting. Something pretty important must have come up for him to stop in midsentence, especially when he was so close to finishing a chapter."

Melody didn't comment. She wondered where on earth was Mr. Hendrick? And her dear aunt? And her best friend Kim? Did some Cobras kidnap them? Or, worse yet, kill the three?

Cold chills ran up her back.

Chapter 6

At the hospital, Jordan returned to the examination room after capturing Leo.

Dr. Thompson shook his head. "Let's stop the bleeding and check those new bruises." The doctor patted the examining table with his hand. "Please, climb back up. I heard you just arrested one of the Cobras. Congratulations. He could have really done a lot of damage here."

"I only wish we knew Sonny and Leo's whereabouts."

"Don't be hard on yourself. At least you got one of them. I heard the news a moment ago, and apparently law enforcement really beefed up security to find the escapees."

Jordan felt some relief at the information, although it didn't surprise him. He only wished he could still be helping.

He sat on the table again, as the doctor examined his new scrapes. Jordan wondered how Melody was doing with the emotional events of the day. He told himself the only reason he wanted her safe was because he would want anyone in her situation to be okay. It wasn't because he once loved her. He couldn't still love her. Could he? Of course not! he quickly told himself. The lady made it clear she didn't want him.

After fifteen minutes, Dr. Thompson patted Jordan's

back. "You're one lucky dude. We got the bleeding stopped with no more stitches."

"I noticed."

"No serious new injuries either. You're going to be sore for the next few days from your bruises though."

Jordan went back to the lounge to wait for his ride home. Captain Scott said he would send someone to pick him up. An hour later, the captain himself walked through the revolving glass door. Melody was with him.

Jordan jumped to his feet. "Melody, you're back with us." His heart soared. He rushed to her and hugged her with his good arm. Her long, red hair felt soft to his touch. Even though he didn't want to, he gently pulled from the embrace. "How are you? Who found you? Did you get hurt?"

The questions tumbled from his mouth.

"It's a long story. Captain Scott found me, and I'm fine."

Jordan didn't believe her. She certainly didn't look okay. She nodded, frowned and bit her lip. Her nervous gestures reminded him of when her father died. She'd made the same mannerisms then. *What on earth happened?*

Captain Scott looked at Jordan. "We'll fill you in on the details later. First things first. What happened to you? You look more beat up than when we dropped you off."

Jordan nodded. "I was in a fight with Leo."

Captain Scott and Melody gasped at the same time.

"Are you okay?" Melody's eyebrows swirled into a m shape.

He thought he saw concern on her face which warmed him. "The doc says I'll be fine." He grinned. "Besides, Leo is now captured and back in prison."

Captain Scott laughed and slapped Jordan's back. "Good work!"

Melody smiled. "You're great at your job, like my father was."

He swallowed hard. If she only knew what happened during her father's tragedy….

Jordan cleared his throat. "Fill me in on what took place with you."

Captain Scott spread his arms outward. "We just came from Melody's aunt's home. Someone broke into it, no doubt the Cobras, and her aunt wasn't there. We're still looking for her."

Jordan gulped. *No wonder Melody looks worried!*

He looked at her. "Do you have any idea where she could be?"

Melody shook her head. "None. We even checked the neighborhood. No one has seen her. I'm worried sick."

Captain Scott took off his police cap and fumbled with it in his hands. "Melody's aunt apparently left her home some time ago and a neighbor's husband, Mr. Hendrick, is missing too. We don't necessarily think they're together. However, we don't know either. They could be since they're friends."

"Where shall we look for them?" Jordan wanted to know.

Captain Scott placed his hat back on his head. "Wait a minute. You've got the rest of the day off. Besides, several lawmen are already searching for the two. We've alerted everyone in the area."

Again, Jordan wanted to argue, but he couldn't. He remembered the doctor's orders: He was to get his pain medication prescription filled immediately, go home, take a pill and get some bed rest. He sighed deeply, knowing he couldn't do anything further in the investigation for now. His new injuries raised his agony to a level he could barely tolerate. He would never admit it to anyone.

Jordon pinched the tip of his nose, tightly closed his eyes and then opened them again. "I don't think Melody should go back to her aunt's house alone."

Melody rubbed the back of her neck. "Captain Scott and I already discussed that. I'd stay with Kim, but she's still missing. I wanted to go to Kim's home to check on her. Captain Scott said we'll have time later. I still think—"

"Good idea," Jordan interrupted. "We've got plenty to do right now." The last thing he wanted now was to talk about Kim.

****

Ding.

"I've got a text message." Melody retrieved the phone from her purse, snapped it open and read: *You'd better go home and see your garage.*

What on earth happened now? Could the note be from a Cobra again? She already got one frightening message. She didn't need another. Yet, she knew she needed to get home. Fast.

"Trouble?" Jordan raised his eyebrows.

Even though Jordan asked the question, Melody turned to Captain Scott. "I'm afraid I need to go home and check the garage." She showed the captain the text.

Captain Scott's dark eyebrows rose. "Let's get Jordan's medicine and drop him off first."

"What does the message say?" Jordan asked.

Melody showed the message to him. He shook his

head, then crossed and uncrossed his arms. "I can go with you."

"No," Captain Scott and Melody said in unison.

Captain Scott raised a hand. "I'll update you on what takes place. The doctor said to make sure you get the medicine and some sleep. Come on. The pharmacy is on our way."

Jordan shook his head. "I want to argue, and I thought I'd never say this, but the pain's becoming more intense."

Melody patted his arm. "I'm glad to see good logic has returned."

He grinned.

When Captain Scott got Jordan's medicine and dropped him off at his home, Melody watched Jordan dash up the porch steps. Then he stopped, grinned and waved a good-bye, sending a warm rush throughout her body. She almost forgot how handsome he looked when he smiled wide, flashing teeth.

Captain Scott looked at her. "Now, let's get back to your aunt's house and see what's up."

"Right." Melody knew she needed to face whatever waited for them.

Moments later, the captain pulled into the driveway of Aunt Sharon's house. Neither Melody nor Captain Scott wasted any time getting out of the car and going inside.

In the entryway, Melody retrieved another letter from the mail. Like the other one, this envelope didn't have a stamp or return address. It must be the message she'd been so anxious to get, ever since she read the text. She ripped it open.

"Hey, you should have put on some gloves first,"

Captain Scott said.

Her head jerked up to see the captain's face. "I'm so sorry. I forgot."

"It's okay. At least we have one letter without your fingerprints."

"So, it's all right if I go ahead and read it?"

"Yes."

She read: *Lots of action happenin.' Be alert.*

What did that mean? She showed it to the captain.

He nodded. "I'll keep this note too, if you don't mind."

"Of course not. Let's get to the garage."

"Right." Captain Scott led the way.

When they entered the carport, Melody exclaimed, "Oh no!"

Gang members apparently slashed Melody's car tires and smashed the vehicle's windows. She'd made her last car payment and was so proud she owned the vehicle now.

On the wall, in red paint, someone wrote: *You gonna die, bitch!*

Beneath the line, gang members apparently sprayed gang-related symbols in black paint.

Melody turned to Captain Scott. "They mean me."

Gently, the captain escorted her back to the kitchen. "We're gonna protect you."

Melody looked at him. "I don't know what I would have done without you today."

"And the police force doesn't know what we would have done without you. You're one brave person, just like your father." Captain Scott shook his head. "You'll never know how much I thought of him."

She smiled.

At the thought of her dad, tears came to her eyes. She missed him so much. She felt his presence now. She knew her father would be proud of her actions today and that gave her strength. Did she have enough courage to face whatever the future held?

When the landline rang, Melody jumped.

It was as though Captain Scott read her mind. "Go ahead and answer. Just keep your cool. No matter who it is, I'll be here with you."

Melody picked up the phone receiver.

"Hello."

"Melody, please forgive me."

Melody's jaw dropped. "Aunt Sharon! Where have you been? We've been looking everywhere for you. Are you okay?"

"I'm fine, dear. How are you? Where are you at? I heard about the riot just now on the news. I'm so sorry you were one of the hostages."

"Yes, Auntie, everything's good." Melody couldn't help it. She started crying, because she was so glad to hear from her aunt. She looked at Captain Scott. "It's Aunt Sharon."

Captain Scott's mouth gaped open. "Is she all right?"

Melody nodded yes as she stayed on the phone.

"Are you still at the prison?" her aunt was asking.

"No, I'm home and with Captain Scott."

"You're safe then?"

"Yes. Right now I want to hear about you. Where are you?"

"I'm at the Hendricks."

"Captain Scott and I just came from there, and Mr. Hendrick wasn't there."

"He's home now. I'm with him and his wife."

"Is he okay? His wife was worried sick about him. Captain Scott and I went to the Hendricks to see if we could find you, and then Mrs. Hendrick told us her husband wasn't anywhere in sight."

"I was with him," Aunt Sharon said. "I'm so sorry we left her. I didn't think to ask Mr. Hendrick if he'd left his wife a note."

"Where have you two been?" Melody was getting impatient.

"At the church to make funeral arrangements. Mr. Buckman passed away. It was a sudden fatal heart attack. The news hit me hard. It happened so fast."

"I'm sorry, Auntie."

Still standing nearby, Captain Scott frowned. "What is it?"

Melody held her hand over the mouthpiece. "One of Aunt Sharon's friends died. They'd gone to high school together."

Captain Scott nodded in understanding as she continued to listen to her aunt, who was saying, "Mr. Hendrick called me several hours ago and asked if I could come right away."

Melody signed. "I'm relieved you and Mr. Hendrick are both safe."

"I didn't mean to worry you."

"Nonsense," Melody said in a forgiving tone. "I can see where you could forget to leave a note under those circumstances. I know you were good friends with Mr. Buckman and his wife. I'm sure you were very upset when you left here. Why didn't his wife Ashley go with you too?"

"Mr. Hendrick thought it would be too much for her

to handle right now. He wanted to tell her the news after he saw Mr. Buckman's wife."

"Doesn't that sound a little strange?" Melody asked.

"Not really. Since I've been volunteering for the grief support group, people can do some odd things after someone dies, especially if the death was sudden."

Melody sighed. "I suppose so. I'm just glad the two of you are safe. I'm sorry about the circumstances though."

"Mr. Buckman and I knew each other for over fifty years. I'm really going to miss him. At least his wife is still with us. I'm leaving the Henricks now and coming home."

"Wait—"

Melody sighed and looked at the captain. "She hung up. She's on her way here. I'm afraid I didn't have a chance to tell her someone broke into our home."

"Then call her back."

Melody shook her head. "She never answers her phone when she's driving."

"Good idea. Then text her."

Melody sent the text. She looked at Captain Scott. "I doubt if she'll see this until she gets home. She's a pretty safe driver."

"Well, we'll be here when she comes," the captain spoke in a caring voice. "We can tell her then. We can meet her at the door."

Suddenly, Melody felt numb from all the events happening. She paced the white tile floor. Back and forth, back and forth. She bit her lip. Finally, after what seemed an eternity, she heard a car approaching. Melody and Captain Scott dashed outside to meet Aunt Sharon.

In seconds, Sharon jumped out of her blue Nissan

and approached her niece. "Hi Captain Scott. Thanks for taking care of my niece."

"Actually she took care of us."

"Oh?" Aunt Sharon frowned.

The captain nodded. "We'll talk about her bravery later. Right now, we've got some bad news."

Melody frowned. "I'm afraid someone broke into the house, auntie. Your things are thrown about in the bedroom."

"It also looks like some guy escaped from the window. Several police are here investigating." Captain Scott nodded.

"Oh dear!" Aunt Sharon flung her hands to her face and headed for the living room. "Do you think it was some escaped convicts?"

The captain grabbed Sharon's arm. "Looks like it. Let's allow the police to do their work."

"Right," Melody agreed. "We don't want to get in their way."

The captain cleared his throat. "There's more to the story."

Sharon turned sharp to face him. "Oh?"

Melody chimed in, "Your garage's a mess. Apparently, some gang members got in."

Sharon's face turned white. "But, but, but, now what?"

Melody worried about her aunt's heart condition. "We'll figure it out. Right now, let's have Captain Scott take us to the hospital and have a doctor check your blood pressure. It's been up the last several weeks. Maybe he can give you a sedative. You've faced an awfully lot of bad news for one day."

Captain Scott rubbed his jaw. "What a great idea.

I'll let the other officers know where we're going. They can finish with the fingerprints."

Sharon raised her arms up. "Nonsense! I won't hear of it. I'm fine."

"No! That's nonsense," Melody wanted her aunt to know. "You've been through a lot today. Come on. You're seeing the doctor."

"Oh, Melody. There's no need for such a thing. Besides, my family doctor is on vacation."

Melody gave an exasperated sigh. "I'm sure another doctor will be able to see you. Listen, one of the reasons I wanted to move back here from Virginia was to look after you, and you encouraged me to do that. So, I'm going to help you now. I'm not giving you a choice on this one."

"Okay, okay." Sharon's arms lowered to her side. "Sometimes you make a good point. I'll only go under two conditions."

Melody crossed her arms and raised an eyebrow. "I hope those conditions are reasonable."

Her aunt smiled. "Of course. I want to call the doctor first."

"No problem. What's the other condition?"

"We drop some of my leftover homemade noodle soup at Jordan's house."

"Which presents an issue," Melody confessed.

"Why? Goodness knows, the man's dealt with enough activity for one day, and he won't feel like preparing his supper. You know how men are. After a stressful day of police work, my husband and your father wouldn't have made a meal for themselves."

Melody remembered. "Good point. Still, I don't think missing one meal is going to hurt Jordan."

"Why, Melody, what's come over you?"

Melody didn't want to say, but the fact was she didn't know if she could face seeing Jordan again. She needed to deal with emotions swirling in her right now.

Captain Scott grinned. "It's a great idea. I'd like to make sure Jordan's safe too. We don't know yet if there's still some escaped convicts after him."

Melody faced the policeman. "Whose side are you on?"

"This isn't a matter of taking sides. I just think it would be good for Jordan to get something to eat, and your aunt knows him well."

"See there." Beaming, Sharon nodded her head.

Moments later, Captain Scott retrieved the pot of homemade soup and a bag of homemade chocolate chip cookies, which Sharon also instructed him to bring.

Guilt overwhelmed Melody. She'd only been thinking of herself. She needed to think of others. Besides, she remembered how Jordan loved her aunt's cooking, especially her homemade soups.

Outside, dark clouds formed, weakening the sunlight. A light rain began to fall and thunder rumbled.

The three settled in the captain's car and Sharon punched the wellness clinic number on her cell phone menu. "Hi. This is Sharon O'Brien. Could I come in to have my blood pressure taken in about an hour? I'm afraid my niece's worried about me, and she thinks I may need a sedative.... You need to get a doctor? Very well. I'll hold."

A moment later, Dr. Thompson was on the phone. "Sure, Mrs. O'Brien, you can come in. Are you free now?"

"I'd rather wait a bit. I'm taking some homemade

soup to one of our policemen. He hurt his arm today and won't feel like cooking. He's a bachelor and the nicest man you'll ever meet. He needs some company now. In fact, I think it would do me some good too. Oh, wait a minute. What happened to my memory? I'm talking about a man you saw today."

"You must be speaking of Lieutenant Lakewater."

"Yes."

"How is he?"

"I think he needs some homemade noodle soup right now. Can I come in later?"

"Sure. Then I can get an update from you on Jordan. I'll be here until late this evening."

"Thanks." Sharon pushed the end button on her call. She took a deep breath and turned to face everyone. "What if Jordan ate supper after all?"

Melody laughed. "You're the one who reminded me Jordan wouldn't feel like preparing a meal. You worry too much."

Sharon gave another sigh. "Well, you must admit, it's been an unusual day."

Melody looked at her aunt. "True."

Captain Scott said, "Hold it, girls."

"What's wrong?" Melody frowned.

"Look behind me. See the black sedan."

"Not again!" Melody exclaimed in alarm.

"Let's not panic," the captain advised. "I hate to break a rule again. Still, if that's the Cobras, I've got to stop them now."

"What's the matter?" Sharon asked.

Captain Scott eased to the side of the road and allowed a car to pass. Then he turned on his siren.

"What's happening?" Sharon inquired again.

Melody heard the concern in her aunt's voice. "Don't worry. Captain Scott is just playing it safe."

The sedan slowly pulled over.

"Right." Captain Scott got out of the car. "I want everyone to be safe. Hang tight."

Chapter 7

Inside Jordan's apartment, he sprawled on the black, leather, sofa bed in the living room. The fresh sheets felt good against his aching body. He'd been able to sleep for a couple hours, which did him a world of good, more than he could have ever imagined. Waiting for the early evening news, he tried to relax by surveying his artwork, hanging everywhere. Pictures of children, flowers, sunsets, and other scenes surrounded the room, giving a homey atmosphere which Jordan loved.

Art was a hobby, and he either hung the pictures he painted, or he gave them to friends or a charity. He began the artwork after suffering from a series of relationships, ending badly. Always picking the wrong woman, he never found one to marry and settle down with, except for Melody, of course. She seemed so right for him. Apparently, she wasn't interested. Boy, she'd made that clear when she said she could never marry a policeman. So, why on earth was she working at the penitentiary as a case manager? He wouldn't concentrate on those things now. He wanted to let go of the past. He refocused on the art.

With the rain pounding on the roof, his paintings comforted him.

When the news began, Jordan punched his unmute button on the remote.

The newscaster reported, "A prison riot occurred

today at McAlester, Oklahoma, the state's only maximum security prison. Three guards, who were stabbed, have now died after being transferred to St. Francis Hospital in Tulsa."

Jordan propped higher on his pillow to focus on the story.

Ten minutes later, regular programming returned and the doorbell rang. He snapped off the television. He wondered who came. Several coworkers stopped by earlier to offer support, and he appreciated their concern more than he could say.

"Alexandria, will you please get the door?" he asked his sister.

"Certainly." She smiled at him.

Jordan remembered how kind his only sister was to him. She arrived at his apartment moments ago. Happy she flew in from Dallas to help him, Jordan also admired her husband, a pilot, who flew her in his private Cessna and then went back to Dallas to return to work.

Alexandria's long, black hair swung as she proceeded to the veranda entrance.

From his sofa bed in the living room, Jordan heard Alexandria exclaim, "Aunt Sharon, Melody, Captain Scott! How great to see all of you!" It was obvious, from the "ohs" and "ahs" he heard, everyone was hugging.

Seconds later, the group entered the living room.

At the sight of Melody, Jordan's heart soared. Now how could he be so happy to see her again? The question troubled him, because in his heart he knew their relationship ended long ago.

Alexandria pulled out several chairs and scooted them by Jordan's side of the bed. "Please, everyone sit down and make yourselves comfortable."

****

As Melody settled in one of the walnut chairs, covered with a thick cushion, she noted Jordan's sparkling, dark eyes. He wore a brown, gym suit with a touch of orange trim, complimenting his skin coloring.

She gave Jordan a weak smile. She hoped he didn't feel like they were intruding. When Jordan grinned wide, Melody could tell he was happy to see her. Good. Of course, on second thought, perhaps she misinterpreted his behavior. Maybe he appeared cheerful simply because he was glad to see her aunt. Perhaps he didn't care if he ever saw her again. She remembered only too well how she turned down his marriage proposal. Even if she broke off the relationship, she hoped, at the time, he would have at least called later and told her good-bye before she left for Virginia. She remembered how she'd wanted to phone and tell him that he would always carry a special place in her heart. She never found enough courage though.

Jordan pulled himself to a sitting position. "Well now, to what do I owe this nice surprise?"

"You've got to eat, young man." Aunt Sharon took the pot of soup from Captain Scott. "I'll warm up some of this right now. We would have been here sooner, but the captain wanted to check out a creepy-looking, black sedan."

"Trouble?" Jordan looked at his boss.

"No, fortunately, it turned out to be nothing. The car was just similar to what the Cobras were driving.

Jordan nodded. "I see."

Alexandria took the pot of soup from Sharon. "Here, let me do that. How kind of you. Jordan hasn't eaten anything for lunch."

"It's chicken noodle." Aunt Sharon looked at Jordan. "I hope you still love it."

"I do, and yours is the best. You brought enough for an army though." Jordan laughed.

"Which was from our leftovers the other night." Melody chuckled.

Jordan looked at Melody's aunt. "You haven't changed. I've really missed you."

Moments later, Alexandria came back to the living room. "Everything's ready. Jordan, do you feel like sitting at the table, or should I bring you a bowl of soup in here?"

Aunt Sharon opened her mouth. Before her aunt could say anything, Jordan was on his feet. "I'd love to go to the table. Then maybe I can keep visiting with everyone before my pain medication kicks in and makes me really sleepy. I just took another pill."

Sharon closed her mouth and said nothing. Melody was relieved, because she knew what her aunt was thinking. She could see the wheels clicking. Aunt Sharon was about to suggest Jordan and Melody eat in the living room by themselves. Her aunt's match-making techniques could be downright embarrassing at times.

Rising from her chair, Melody trailed to the kitchen with everyone else. There, a red tablecloth graced the table, displayed in front of a bay window that Melody remembered well. How often Jordan and she'd sat at the bay window as they ate hot fudge sundaes. The favorite dessert was one of the many things they shared in common.

The rain fell hard outside, and lightning sliced across the sky.

"This table looks beautiful!" Sharon exclaimed.

"You really outdid yourself."

Alexandria laughed. "I want to give you guys a chance to visit. I know it's been a long time. I'm just thrilled to see all of you."

Melody sighed. "I'm afraid we can't stay long. I'm taking Aunt Sharon to the doctor."

Alexandria frowned as she swung her hair back. "I understand. Aunt Sharon, I hope you're doing well."

Sharon flipped her hand nonchalantly in the air. "I'm fine. Just need to have my hypertension checked is all."

Jordan looked at her. "A good idea. You've dealt with a lot today."

Sharon smiled. "You sound exactly like my niece."

While Melody waited to take her place at the table, Jordan came behind her, quickly took her hand and escorted her to the seat next to him. Was this really happening? Did he want to sit by her? Or did her aunt whisper in Jordan's ear to do the kind act?

He pulled out a chair for her.

"Thank you." She took the seat.

Jordon settled beside her and gave her hand a quick squeeze. Sharon, sitting at the opposite end, lifted one eyebrow above her glasses. It didn't take a psychologist to see her aunt was having the time of her life. Melody hoped Aunt Sharon never said anything to Jordan about making sure they sat side by side.

****

Jordan glanced up and grinned, thinking how fortunate he was to be with everyone at the table.

"Who can I help first?" He grabbed the large soup bowl with both arms. Immediately, he placed the heavy bowl back on the table. "Ouch!"

Melody wheezed. "Be careful."

Alexandria stood up, picked up the dish and placed it in front of her. "I'll do the serving. You've got an injured arm. Remember?" She glared at her brother.

Jordan knew what the look meant. He'd seen it before when Alexandria got impatient with him, which was not often.

He chuckled. "Sorry, I'm afraid I forgot about my arm."

Alexandria smiled and sat back down.

Melody's nearness left a lump in Jordan's throat. How often they sat side by side, laughing and enjoying life. Everything was so different now.

Moments later, his sister placed hot bowls of soup in front of everyone. Then she passed a large platter of cheddar cheese and crackers around the table. Jordan tasted the warm chicken noodle soup. The homemade wide noodles, carrots and thick chicken broth tasted better than he even remembered.

"Aunt Sharon, this is absolutely delicious! Between this and my medicine, I'm in a good mood." He didn't say anything further, but having Melody by his side made him even happier.

Sharon dabbed her mouth with a napkin. "Thanks, Jordan. You have no idea how much I missed making it for you." She cleared her throat. "You never explained why you stopped visiting me."

"I thought I did." Jordan chuckled, remembering how mischievous Aunt Sharon could be when she wanted to clear the air about something. He admitted silently he couldn't bear the thought of seeing Aunt Sharon after Melody left. He knew that was poor behavior on his part. After all, Melody's aunt treated him like a son. Why, if it wasn't for her, he'd no doubt still be getting in trouble, like he was in his teen years. He should have kept in touch with Aunt Sharon, regardless of what happened between him and her niece.

Sharon smiled slyly. "Actually, you didn't explain why you stopped seeing me."

Melody fumbled with an earring she wore. "Past history. Auntie, you don't need an explanation."

Jordan rubbed his hands nervously on his jeans, and his mouth twisted into a grimace. He could tell he'd hurt Melody's aunt. "Aunt Sharon, I apologize. I'm sorry. If it weren't for you I'd be out there with some of those gang members, rather than being a police officer. You saved me from such fate."

Sharon waved her hand. "Nonsense. If it wasn't for me, someone else would have reached out to you."

Jordan shook his head. "I'm not so sure."

Sharon smiled and looked his way. "Jordan, hon, this fine community is larger than a lot of people may think. Someone would have given you the appropriate guidance in your life. You're the type of person everyone loves."

Alexandria smiled. "I agree. I've got a great brother. He's simply trying to thank you for everything you did for him. We've talked many times about how you helped both of us. Our mother cared more about her alcohol than either Jordan or me."

Jordan squirmed in his seat. He never revealed much about his mother to Melody, other than to say his mother spent more time drunk than sober.

He rose from his chair. "I'm sorry for not seeing you after Melody moved to Virginia. I really am. Will you ever forgive me?"

He spread out his arms. Tears flowed down Sharon's puffy cheeks.

"Of course, son." She embraced him in a tight hug.

Jordan noted it wasn't the first time Aunt Sharon called him son. She always called him that when he and Melody were a twosome. His heart warmed at the sound of the word coming once again from her mouth. How could he have ignored this fine lady? How could he tell her now that when Melody left him, everything fell to pieces in his world? He couldn't think straight at the time, and he'd feared seeing her aunt would be more than he could handle.

After the hug, Jordan returned to his seat.

Sharon wiped the tears from her eyes. "Having you come back into my life today is such a blessing. Melody and I need you now more than ever."

"Aunt Sharon!" Melody exclaimed in a scolding voice. "I think the man has quite enough to do other than looking out for the two of us."

Jordan's heart dropped. Could the woman make it any more obvious she still didn't want anything more to do with him? He needed to leave her alone or else she'd break his heart all over again. Which was the last thing he wanted.

The next hour was an enjoyable one of visiting with everyone, still seated at the table.

Captain Scott's cell phone rang.

The captain retrieved the cell from his pocket and snapped it open. "Please excuse me." He said several "uh hums" intermingled with some "yeses" and then added, "I'll be right there."

Snapping his cell shut, he rose from his chair.

"Everyone, please forgive me. I've got to run right now. Duty calls."

Chapter 8

Being off work for three days, at the captain's insistence, Jordan felt nearly normal when he got up early, Tuesday morning. After dressing, he went to the kitchen and sat at the table to enjoy a scrambled eggs, potatoes, bacon and biscuit breakfast his sister prepared for him. Heartily, he dug in.

"I'm glad to see you've got your appetite back." Alexandria smiled and set a cup of steaming hot chocolate, piled with whipped cream, in front of him.

He nodded. "Thanks. I appreciate your help more than I can say."

"Did you sleep well?"

He took a gulp of the liquid and laughed. "The pain meds knocked me out this weekend. I don't think I've ever slept so good."

"Great. You needed the rest."

"Yeah." He nodded towards the television on the wall in front of the table. "Mind if I watch the news?"

"Of course not."

His sister snapped on the TV, and when Alexandria returned to her seat, Jordan punched the remote. They sat through a couple commercials before the news came on.

The news anchor said, "A McAlester resident was captured only an hour ago, after robbing a Wilburton convenience store. Law enforcement officials picked up Tony McFarris, 38, after receiving a 911 call, made by one of the store employees at 3:30 a.m. this morning. Authorities took McFarris, a Cobra gang member, to the Pittsburg County jail. McFarris moved to McAlester about a month ago and worked at a local grocery. Authorities think McFarris may have connections with two prisoners, Allen Shiver and Sonny Furemore, who remain at large, after escaping from the Oklahoma State Prison in McAlester."

Jordan almost dropped his cup of chocolate. Instead, he weakly set the mug on the table.

"So, other Cobras are in McAlester, besides the prison. Exactly what we were afraid of."

"Oh no." Alexandria spoke in a soft voice.

The reporter continued. "Shiver is 33 years old, stands 6 feet 2 inches tall, weighs 175 pounds and has brown hair and eyes. He is heavily tattooed and has two piercings, one by his left eyebrow and the other on his nose. Furemore, who is 51, is 5 feet 8 inches tall and weighs 310 pounds. He has black hair, partially gray, with long sideburns and a gold front tooth. Both men are extremely dangerous and may be armed."

After breakfast, Jordan drove to the police station himself, since he was no longer on pain medication. There, he poured a cup of coffee and settled behind his desk in the corner. Several sun rays shone on a greenery plant, and the tiny, yellow flowers sparkled in the sunlight.

He took a gulp of coffee and knew the time had come to call Kim. He retrieved his cell, punched in the contact and took a deep breath, as he waited for her to answer.

"Hello." The answer came on the third ring.

"Hi Kim, it's Jordan."

"Hi. It's nice to hear your voice."

"Listen, we've got to talk. Can you meet me somewhere?"

"Sure. Where would you like to go?"

"Somewhere private. Very private."

Jordan made arrangements to meet at a new café and then said good-bye to Kim and hung up the phone.

He leaned back in his chair. The restaurant set in a wooded area on the outskirts of McAlester. Surely, Kim and he could have a conversation there without anyone seeing or hearing them.

Chapter 9

Later in the evening, Melody tossed and turned in bed. Her aunt needed to remain in the hospital for observation and blood pressure monitoring. The doctors suspected she may need heart surgery and were giving her a bunch of tests. Somehow the place didn't seem the same without her dear relative. Finally Melody fell asleep. Thirty minutes passed.

Bang!

She awoke, her heart racing at the sudden noise. Her muscles tensed. Struggling for breath, she jerked to an upright position. Did the noise come from a gunshot? What if a gang member prowled outside, trying to get her? What if it was Sonny and Allen?

She retrieved her gun from the bedstand drawer, slipped out of bed and crept to the window. Slowly, she pulled the drapes back just enough to see the backyard. She thought she saw something dark to the right side, but when she turned her head, she saw nothing. She heard another sound, like a cat clawing at her window. Perhaps it was someone's pet who'd run off. Being a middle-class neighborhood, a lot of residents in the area owned animals. Scanning the yard for a cat or dog, she didn't see any four-legged creatures.

She waited for a long time. She didn't hear any more noises. She shook her head and concluded she'd been dreaming. She placed the weapon back in the drawer, climbed in bed and finally drifted to asleep. Thirty minutes later, she awoke to find a man standing by her bed. With the nightlight on, she recognized him. It was Allen.

She screamed.

"Get out of bed," he hissed.

Melody's heart lurched in her chest. Paralyzed with fear, she wasn't sure she could move. Allen snatched a .45 caliber auto from his pocket and aimed the weapon at her.

"Move!" he shouted.

Melody jumped out of bed.

He grinned wickedly. "You're coming with me."

"No, no, no, please don't."

Tossing his head back, Allen gave a raucous laugh. His Adam's apple bobbed up and down in the darkened room, illuminated by slivers of moonlight shining through the window.

Melody clutched her arms around her shaking body. "Just tell me what you need."

"I need you!" He pushed the pistol into her stomach. He held a large can with his other arm. She didn't have a chance to see any identification on the container. What was he holding? Beads of sweat formed on her forehead and in the palms of her hands. She gave an involuntary puff.

Her mind racing, Melody tried to think of a way to escape. "What about my clothes? I need to get some."

"I'm not stupid, baby doll. If I let you get some clothes, you'd just escape."

"Well, I'm not about to freeze to death. I'm getting a coat."

"Okay, grab a jacket. Just remember, I'm following

you every inch of the way." Allen turned sharp and jabbed his gun into her back. Melody shivered as she dashed to the living room closet. She could have retrieved an outer garment from her bedroom, but she wanted to stall Allen to attempt a safe escape. She fought emotionally to think of some way to stop all the madness. Slowly, she walked to living room.

Allen followed, keeping the gun pressed to her back. "Hurry. Don't take all day!"

She opened the closet door and pulled out a coat.

"Now, we're gonna get in my car and you're not going to scream. Got it?"

Melody's heart hammered, her heart still racing. "I need to put on my coat."

"Hurry then!" He flipped the cold gun to her forehead.

Struggling, Melody slipped into the outerwear with Allen pressing the weapon hard against her skin.

"Walk out the door! Now!" he demanded, flipping the weapon against her back again.

Outside, Melody prayed some neighbor would be up and see them. No such luck. Still shoving the .45 against her back, Allen pushed her to a green and beat-up SUV. With his free hand, he yanked the door open.

"Get in!" He hissed the order.

He shoved her inside, slammed the door shut and locked it. He raced back toward the house.

Allen smashed the front living room window and jumped inside.

What on earth is he doing?

She couldn't see Allen now, but a moment later, he was back in the car, and hot, red flames burst forth from the living room window.

She cawed. She realized now the can he'd held was gasoline. "You set the house on fire!"

Allen laughed wickedly. "Yeah, you can thank me for saving your life later." He started the SUV and took off.

She glanced out the car window to see the devilish flames raging in the house, a home she'd dearly cherished. Rubbing her temples, she let out a childlike snuffle. Tears fell on her face. She quickly wiped them with the back of her hand before Allen saw her emotions.

Thirty minutes later, in the madness, Allen pulled up to a dilapidated trailer. She'd kept a keen eye on the terrain on the trip and figured they must near Talihina, a town about fifty miles from McAlester. He snapped off the car engine and, using his pistol again, forced her inside. There, Sonny sat in the kitchen. A plate of nachos set in front of him.

When he saw Allen and Melody, Sonny slammed a beer can on the table and leaned back in his chair. "Well, if it isn't Miss America." Sonny glanced at his buddy. "Where'd you ever find her?"

"At her aunt's house, just like we figgered."

Sonny raised his eyebrows. "And is the house burnin' now?"

"Yeah, I'm sorry about not bringing her aunt here. She wasn't home."

Sonny grinned. "No problem, bro."

A relaxed smile crossed Allen's face. "Really?"

Sonny nodded. "Yeah. Think about it. She'd just have been in the way."

Nodding, Allen chuckled. "Ah, I see what you mean, boss."

With his foot, Sonny slid a chair from the table and

nodded at Melody. "Sit down and make yourself at home."

Melody knew it would be no use arguing at this point. Once again she needed to surrender to Sonny. She sat on the chair he'd pulled out for her.

"Start talkin,'" Sonny demanded.

Melody frowned. "About what?"

Sonny took a long swig of beer and wiped some of the foam from the edge of his mouth with the back of his hand. "Your boyfriend. We need information before we gotta do what we gotta do."

"Boyfriend, what boyfriend? I don't have one."

Sonny snickered. "Yeah, you do. The fuzz, Lakewater."

"Jordan?" Melody's heart thumped at the sound of his name.

Sonny nodded. "Right. Allen and I here know the two of you were gonna get hitched some years ago."

"How'd you know?"

Allen took a chair at the small table. "We know everything about you, sweetheart."

"Shut up! I'll do the talkin'." Sonny's eyes bulged.

Shrugging his shoulders, Allen held up his hands. "Hey, man, don't get on my case. You wanted me to find the bitch, and I found her. Now we need information. I don't see wasting no time to—"

"I said, 'Shut up!'"

Melody wondered if Sonny and Allen were holding Kim hostage somewhere too. Or worse, did they kill her?

How was she ever going to get through this? Why did such terrible things happen recently in the first place? From the tiny trailer window, she glanced out into the dark night. Stars hung high in the sky.

Sonny cleared his throat. "We've got to talk to Lakewater. Get some things settled."

Melody's eyes widened. "I don't know where he's at."

"Yes, you do!" Sonny slammed a fist on the table. "You and him were in on this together."

With a mouthful of nachos, Allen interrupted, "So, we didn't need her after all?"

Sonny grinned, showing his gold tooth. "Oh, we need her all right, just not yet. She shot one of our bros. First, we got to get Lakewater though. Come on, help me tie the bitch up. We've got to get the fuzz wherever he's at. Then we'll deal with her."

Melody didn't like what she was hearing at all. It sounded like a lot of Cobras drifted into the McAlester community over the past year.

Allen grinned and then laughed. "Good thinkin,' boss." He took a gulp of beer. "Why don't you call your cousin in Tulsa now? See if he can help us. Tell him we'd much obliged."

"We're a long way from there right now. I'm not sure we could swing that just yet without the police seein' us." Sonny shoved several nachos in his mouth

Allen nodded. "Smart thinkin.'"

Straightening in his chair, Sonny jerked to attention. "Shhhh."

Allen frowned. "What's up?"

Slowly, Sonny pushed a torn curtain aside. "I'm not sure. I think I spotted someone way back in the woods. We've got to get outta here fast."

"Let me see." Allen peeked out the other side of the window. "Where?"

"Off to the right. Way, way back."

"I see 'em!"

Sonny jumped from his chair. "Pack our stuff, while I keep an eye peeled. Someone's walking away from us. As soon as he's outta sight, we'll take off."

"What're we going to do with her?" Allen nodded to Melody.

"Tie her up and hide her, where no one's going to find her."

Melody wanted to protest. She knew it would be no use though and no doubt would get her in more danger than she was already in. The two gang members went into quick drive. Before Melody knew what was happening, they'd wrapped duct tape around her mouth and tied a rope around her hands. Her face grew red hot. She wanted to scream for help. She couldn't. Allen and Sonny drug her to a back bedroom and shoved her under the bed. After a few seconds, she heard the door slam shut on the trailer.

Now what? Will anyone ever find me?

Chapter 10

Meanwhile, Captain Scott asked Jordan to go to the prison with him to interrogate Leo. Jordan wanted to help with the investigation all he could. He felt his job was a special calling and, if they were lucky, Leo just may give them the information needed to find the two escapees.

When they got to the penitentiary, Jordan rushed to the interrogation room with Captain Scott. A prison official greeted them and closed the door. Leo sat on a chair at one of the narrow table ends.

The officer looked at Captain Scott and Jordan and then nodded towards Leo. "He's all yours. I'm going to leave you two. If you need anything, let us know."

Captain Scott grinned. "Thanks."

Jordan nodded to Leo. "Do you want something before we start? Coffee?"

"No, never drink the stuff. I'd like a Coke."

"Okay." Jordan called to the prison secretary in the hallway. "Susan, would you please bring a Coke in here for us?"

"Sure thing." Susan walked down the hall towards the vending machine.

"Just tap on the door when you get here, Susan," Jordan instructed.

"Will do."

Jordan closed the door.

Captain Scott looked at Leo. "You can help us if you

tell us where Allen and Sonny are at."

Shaking his head, Leo looked at Jordan and Captain Scott. "Cobras don't snitch."

There was a tap at the door. The secretary entered with the soda pop.

"Thanks." Jordan took the can.

Susan smiled. "No problem. Need anything else?"

"Yeah," Leo piped up. "Some warm chocolate chip cookies."

Susan shook her head, winked at Jordan and whispered, "Sounds like you've got your work cut out for you."

Jordan gave a weak grin, nodded and closed the door. Still standing, he put the soda down next to his coffee cup and glared at Leo, as if he dared him to reach for the container. Might as well use the liquid refreshment as bait for more information, Jordan figured. Sometimes the tactic worked. Sometimes not. It was worth a try though.

Captain Scott cleared his throat and looked at Leo. "We know you're a Cobra."

"Yeah, man, proud of it too." Leo snickered.

"I suggest you cooperate with us and not get smart," the captain said.

Like Captain Scott, Jordan waited for a response from Leo and got none. Both men stood on the opposite sides of the table.

Jordan took a seat. He saw anger flare in Leo's blue eyes. Jordan could already tell Leo wasn't going to be easy; gang members never were. He'd worked with kids like Leo before, youths who never experienced a good home life, hit the streets and joined a gang to feel a part of something, anything. He remembered only too well how he'd almost been one of those youngsters, and now he wanted to help them. But how? Which was always the question. How could he get through to young men like Leo?

Leo cracked his knuckles. "Ain't nothin' against the law about belonging to a group of bros."

Captain Scott sat down, opposite Leo. "Depends."

Leo frowned. "On what?"

The captain leaned back and sighed. "If the gang commits criminal activity." He spoke calmly.

Leo ignored the comments, and Jordan saw, from Leo's body language, what Captain Scott said hadn't sunk in yet.

"I suggest you start talking."

"Hey, man, I'm just answerin' the questions, like you wanted."

"It's your tone of voice I don't like. You need an attitude adjustment." Captain Scott leaned forward. "Now, where are your buddies, Sonny and Allen?"

Leo shrugged. "Dunno."

Captain Scott yelled, "You're lying!"

"No, I'm not!"

Jordan slammed a fist on the table. "Yes, you are!"

Hanging his head, Leo muttered something inaudible.

"What did you say? We didn't hear you! Speak up!" the captain shouted.

"Nothin, man, I didn't say nothin'." Leo's eyes shifted back and forth.

Leo avoided eye contact with Jordan. He'd learned long ago when a person glanced from one side to the other, the body language was generally a good indication the person wasn't telling the truth.

Captain Scott slapped his hands on the table and yelled within inches of Leo's face. "We know you were with Sonny and Allen at the riot, and you escaped with them."

Leo crossed his arms and snickered. "Oh yeah? Prove it."

"Okay, I will." Jordan seized the moment. He grabbed a large, brown envelope by his chair and pulled out a photo. He tossed the picture on the table. The glossy showed Leo running from the prison grounds with Sonny and Allen.

Leo looked at the photo. His face turned white.

He shook his head. "That's not me."

"Don't be stupid!" Captain Scott kept shouting in Leo's face. "We know you don't have a twin anywhere. Where did you and your two friends go?"

Leo glanced up. "What happens if I don't want to talk?"

Jordan cleared his throat. "You could get a longer prison sentence."

Leo jerked his neck, like a turtle from its shell. "Why?"

Jordan spread his arms on the table and gave Leo eye contact. "For not cooperating, for withholding information."

Shaking his head, Leo sighed, rubbed his hands together and then snapped his knuckles several more times.

Getting up, the captain swirled the chair. Spreading his legs apart, Captain Scott flung one leg over the chair first and then the other. He sat with the back of the chair between Leo and him. "You better start talking."

Leo's hands began shaking. "Look, I'm not going to

snitch on anyone. If Sonny and Allen found out I told on them, they'd cream me when they get back to prison."

Captain Scott looked at Leo. "Doesn't sound like very good friends to me. Now, where are they hiding out?"

"My mouth's shut." Leo shook his head vigorously.

Jordan coughed. "If you don't start telling us something, you'll be in prison a long, long time, maybe for life. Did you know your friends killed three guards in the riot?"

Looking up, Leo's eyes widened at the information. "No. I guess it don't surprise me none. Everything was happenin' so fast."

"Did you kill anyone in the riot?" Captain Scott asked.

"No!"

After a moment of silence, Jordan crossed his arms. "So, tell us, why did you join a gang in the first place?"

Leo shrugged. Jordan could tell he hit a nerve.

Captain Scott folded his hands. "We're waiting."

Still hanging his head, Leo twirled his thumbs around each other. "I-I-I wanted to belong, ya' know."

Jordan nodded and leaned forward. "Actually, I do know what it's like to not have both parents provide a solid home life, to want to be part of something important."

"Why else did you want to join a gang?" Captain Scott asked.

"I didn't have another reason besides belonging." Leo shrugged.

"Well, there should be no problems in prison if you want to belong. A handsome guy like you will have all kinds of men wanting you." Captain Scott grinned slyly at Jordan.

Jordan chuckled. "Right."

Looking up, Leo frowned. "What do ya'all mean?"

Captain Scott surveyed Leo up and down. "Yeah, a young, good looking guy like you will belong there all right, for a long time. Matter of fact, you'll be real popular. You maybe are already."

Leo snorted. "I'm not that kind. Besides just who sez' I'm goin' to stay in prison?"

Captain Scott cleared his throat. "You're facing a lot of hard time if you don't talk. You'd better start telling us every single detail you can remember."

"Oh, yeah. What am I facin'?" Leo's voice quivered.

Captain Scott nodded soberly. "Maybe a life sentence."

Leo jumped to his feet. "Hey, they can't do such a thing to me. I ain't stayin' in here for the rest of my life."

"If you go down alone for the murders you no doubt will."

Spit flew from Leo's mouth. "I'm not guilty! I didn't kill no one."

Captain Scott folded his arms. "Then help us out. If we can't find Sonny and Allen, the officials could blame you for the murders. We can't capture Sonny and Leo and charge them with the killings, if we can't find them."

Leo sat back down and slammed his hands on the table. "Look man, I didn't want no one killed. I just wanted to hang out with Sonny and Allen. They're big stuff in the gang. Okay?"

The captain nodded. "Being a big shot in taking lives isn't what I'd call impressive. Instead, it's downright evil."

"So, tell us where they're at," Jordan requested.

"I-I-I dunno."

"Of course you do! Now spill it," Captain Scott shouted.

"I'm tellin' the truth. I don't know. It's not like I've ever lived with the guys or anything," Allen yelled back. "You know?"

"Of course you lived with them. You were in prison together!" Jordan snapped.

Leo looked at Jordan, doubled his fists and lowered his head. "I don't want any part of this."

The captain leaned forward. "You're in prison now, and you won't ever be seeing Sonny and Allen again, if we have anything to say about it. Your prison cells will be far apart from each other, if Sonny and Allen get on Death Row."

Leo shook his head. "I'm not tattling on my bros."

"Oh, so it looks like you'll be the only one going down for these murders then." Captain Scott sighed.

Jordan realized his boss just nailed Leo. Good move.

Leo snapped his head up like a turtle. "What do ya'll mean?"

"My, my, my, seems like you have a short memory for someone nicknamed Brains." Captain Scott spoke in sarcasm.

"How'd you know my nickname?"

Captain Scott snickered. Jordan knew this was the captain's famous attempt to keep up the intimidation process going, and he was good at it, real good.

Leo blinked back tears for the first time. "I don't want Sonny and Allen to get in trouble 'cause I snitched."

Jordan leaned forward. "You're already in trouble."

"I love Sonny and Leo like brothers. They're like

family, ya' know."

"Well, you'll be responsible if you don't start cooperating. You don't want that." The captain leaned back in his chair.

Leo became visibly shaken. He was pale and his head jerked at intervals. He looked at Jordan and then Captain Scott.

Silence hung in the room for a moment.

"A long sentence isn't fair!" Leo yelled.

"It's the law," Captain Scott shouted. "It's justice."

"Forget the law!" Leo snapped.

"You better watch who you're talking too!" Captain Scott folded his hands and leaned across the table.

"Still, not fair." Leo changed his voice to friendly. "I didn't kill those guards. Sonny and Leo did. I told them not to."

"Then you'd better keep talking and not waste any more of our time," Captain Scott suggested. "Now, where are they at?"

Leo remained silent.

Captain Scott shook his head. "We can't put someone in jail we can't find. Yeah, you'll be serving time for your brothers too. Boy, some loyalty."

Slowly, Leo began giving the location to an abandoned trailer near Talihina, where he thought Sonny and Leo may have escaped to.

Bingo! Thrilled at the information, Jordan handed the soda to Allen. Time for the reward.

Leo took the soda, snapped the top open and took several long gulps.

Captain Scott grinned. Jordan could tell his boss was enjoying this as much as he was. Maybe they could capture Sonny and Allen now.

After Leo gave the directions for the secluded trailer, Jordan and Captain Scott wasted no time to end the interrogation. Jordan knew their work was cut out for them; they needed to arrest Sonny and Allen. Fast. Jordan just hoped Sonny and Allen were staying at the Talihinia trailer, that Leo was telling the truth. And, Jordan also hoped that Sonny and Allen were home.

Chapter 11

An hour later, near Talihina, rain poured in sheets as Jordan and Captain Scott swiftly dashed from one tree to the next in the wooded area.

Captain Scott puffed. "I didn't realize we'd get such a workout tonight. How's your arm holding up?"

"Not so bad."

"Glad to hear it."

Jordan thought of his bed back home and how he'd like more shut eye, but he needed to go on. He couldn't give up. Not when Sonny and Allen were still missing, and Leo may have just given them the information they needed to catch the guys. He rushed from one tree to the next with the captain. Thirty minutes passed with no results. The rain kept pouring, stinging Jordan's back, face and arms. The discomfort especially rose in his injured arm. In spite of it, he kept moving.

Suddenly, Jordan spotted a long, white rectangle in the dark.

He pointed. "Look, captain, isn't that what we're looking for?"

"Sure looks like it. We'd better be careful as we approach the building. Everything's dark. They're probably in there hiding, and I'm sure they're armed."

"My thoughts exactly."

Even with the bad weather, the timing of the police search party turned out great, Jordan realized. Law enforcement in the search unit now approached the cabin with them, arriving at the same time.

"Police!" Jordan and Captain Scott yelled, as they burst open the door.

In seconds, Jordan, Captain Scott and several other officers were inside. They searched the trailer and found no one.

Captain Scott rubbed his hands together. "Everyone, listen up. We've got to keep searching." He called out the names of several officers. "I'll have you guys immediately get in your cars and search. Sonny and Allen apparently left in a big hurry."

Jordan scratched the back of his neck. "Yeah, I noticed. The nachos are half-eaten, and the beer cans are half full too."

The other officers headed out the door to search for the two gang members.

"I'll go too," Jordan volunteered.

The captain shook his head no. "I'm sorry. I can't let you."

Jordan frowned. "Why not?"

"Your arm. I promised Dr. Thompson I'd take good care of you, and I meant it. You've already stretched yourself pretty thin. Besides, someone needs to stay here in case Sonny and Allen come back."

Jordan shook his head. "You make a good point, captain. Okay then, I'll stay."

"Good, I'm keeping two other policemen, Joe and Kevin, with you, just in case Allen and Sonny come back here. Plus, there'll be several more officers outside near the trailer. You can lie down and get more rest with the other guys on the watch."

Jordon nodded and didn't argue. "I appreciate it."

The captain grinned. "I was afraid you were going to put up a fight, say you needed to stay up too."

Jordan grinned. "I'd have both you and the doctor on my case if I didn't follow orders. Besides, the other men are more than capable of handling things."

Captain Scott chuckled. "Exactly." He turned toward Joe and Kevin, now standing by them. "You guys let Jordan sleep all he can."

Joe nodded. "Don't worry. We've got his back."

"Yes," Kevin agreed.

Jordan placed his hands on his hips. "I'll still be here to help you if they come back."

Kevin looked at Jordan. "Sounds good."

Jordan nodded. "If it's okay, I'm going to lie down now."

Captain Scott headed for the door. "No problem. Get all the rest you can."

Jordan trailed to a back bedroom. When he lied on the bed, he felt something. What was it?

He jumped off the bed. "Come in here, captain."

"What's the matter?" Captain Scott raced down the hallway.

Jordan looked at the captain, now in the bedroom. "Did you hear something, like a thud?"

"I think so."

Thud. Thud, thud. Jordan saw the bed move with each thud. "See what I mean?"

"Yeah, I do. What is it?"

Before Jordan could answer, the captain lifted the mattress with both hands and shoved it against a wall. There, on the floor, Melody curled in a knot, still with her hands and feet bounded with rope and her mouth taped shut.

"Oh, no!" Jordan and his boss said in unison. Joe and Kevin ran into the room.

Jordan looked at Melody. "Thank goodness, you're alive!"

"Yes!" Captain Scott laughed with Jordan.

Tears streamed across Melody's oval-shaped face. Her eyes were wide.

"Hold on, this is going to sting a little." Jordan began pulling duct tape off her mouth with his good arm, with the captain's help, while Joe and Kevin removed the rope around her hands and feet and helped her to stand up.

Melody gave a quick jump. "Thank you, guys!" She rubbed her wrists. Jordan gently kissed her on the forehead. Her skin was soft, warm, inviting to his lips.

"We had no idea you were here," the captain exclaimed.

"How long were you bound up?" Jordan gave her hand a quick squeeze.

She shook her head. "I'm not sure, maybe thirty minutes. It seemed like forever. I was terrified. Someone's got to look for Sonny and Allen. They were here just a few minutes ago."

"Do you have any idea which direction they headed?" Jordan asked.

Melody took a deep breath. "I'm afraid not. The rain was pouring so loud on the roof, I couldn't hear the car take off. I just heard the door slam. Then all I heard was the storm outside."

Jordan and the captain shook their heads at the same time.

The captain immediately radioed the information to the rest of the officers and issued orders for a dozen guys to take off in police cars in different directions to look for the two gang members. Then he looked at Melody. "What happened anyway?"

Jordan raked his hands through his black hair. "Yeah, how'd you get here?"

Melody folded her arms. "Allen set fire to my aunt's house and brought me here. Fortunately, Aunt Sharon's still in the hospital. Do you know how much damage was done to our home?"

At the news, Jordan bent his neck forward, and then he straightened. "No, we don't know. We were at the prison."

The captain rubbed his neck. "Yeah, we were interrogating Leo. We didn't even know about the fire. Leo just gave us a tip that Sonny and Allen may be here, and we headed off to this area right away."

"I'm so glad you guys found me. I'm worried about my aunt. Has she heard about her house burning?"

Jordan shrugged and spread his arms. "We don't know."

"Let's go see her," the captain suggested.

Melody sighed. "How am I ever going to tell my aunt her home was destroyed, and I was taken hostage? She's trying to get her blood pressure down, not up."

Captain Scott took off his police cap, scratched his head and then plopped the hat back on his head. "Still, we've got to give her the news before the media does, if they haven't already."

Melody nodded in agreement.

The three of them left to see Aunt Sharon, while other officers in the search party stayed with Kevin and Joe to be on the lookout for Sonny and Allen.

At the hospital, Jordan raced down the hallway

between the captain and Melody. With Melody by his side, he felt relieved and shuddered at the thought of the narrow escape from danger she just experienced. He needed to protect her. That was the least he could do after what happened to her father.

Automatically, the three trailed down the hall.

Seconds later, in Aunt Sharon's room, the doctor tucked his stethoscope in his pocket and nodded at the three of them. Still wearing her nightgown and coat, Melody gave the doctor a weak smile.

Dr. Thompson frowned. "What on earth is going on?"

Aunt Sharon bolted upright. "The three of you look troubled. What is it? What happened?"

Melody nodded. "Doctor, this is Captain Scott, and you've already seen Lieutenant Lakewater."

The doctor shook the captain's hand and then looked at Jordan. "Yes. How are you, Jordan?"

"Good, Doc. I got some rest, then duty called."

The doctor frowned and looked back at Melody. "What's wrong? You look like you just lost your best friend."

Aunt Sharon straightened in the bed. "Oh my, you do look sad, all three of you." Nervously, she tucked at her flowered, lounge gown. "If it makes you feel any better, my blood pressure is exactly where it's supposed to be, and I can go home tomorrow morning."

The doctor nodded. "And the time will be here before we know it. I normally wouldn't allow visitors at this time, but they look like they have something important to tell you."

Melody gave a weak nod. "We do. Doctor, you probably need to stay. I've got some bad news, and I'm concerned about my aunt's blood pressure when she hears everything."

The doctor nodded. "I hear you."

Melody sat on the edge of the bed and hugged her aunt. "I don't know how to tell you everything."

Aunt Sharon's eyebrows shot up. "Just tell me. What happened? After what we've been through, it couldn't be so bad."

Jordan cleared his throat. "I want to help Melody tell you the news, but I don't know how." Gently, he sat down near the bed. He took the older lady's hand and kissed it. "Brace yourself."

Aunt Sharon took Jordan's hand. "What is it, son?"

****

The word son warmed Melody's heart. Her aunt still thought the world of the guy and Melody understood why. Jordan was the kindest and most caring man she'd ever met. Her heart ached. She could never be with him the way things were. She'd fight off the new feelings in her heart, stirrings, longing for Jordan again to be the man in her life.

"I'm afraid something terrible has happened to your home…" Melody began and stopped.

Sharon grabbed her niece's hands. "What? Another break in? Did someone destroy a bunch of my things, like they destroyed your car?"

Melody shook her head. "It's worse. There was a fire in your home…"

"A fire!" Aunt Sharon jerked her hands from Melody, flung her arms high and then let them flop on the bed. "How bad was it?"

Dr. Thompson rushed to Sharon. "Please, Mrs. O'Brien, try to take this calmly. Okay? However harmful the fire was, we'll get through it."

Sharon nodded faintly and laid back on her pillow.

Melody fought back the tears. She looked at Jordan.

Jordan leaned towards Sharon. "Melody just told me about it on the way here, and I called the fire officials right away to get the facts. We don't even have all the details yet. I'm afraid your house...well..."

"Just tell me."

Tears streamed down the older lady's cheeks.

Her dear aunt must be in terrible shock right now. And Melody knew Jordan struggled for a way to tell her, a way to soften the words, make the situation less dramatic for Aunt Sharon. But how?

She took her aunt's hands. "I'm afraid your precious home has been destroyed."

"Oh no! How did the fire start?" Sharon jerked back to an upright sitting position.

Melody burst into tears and let go of her aunt's hands. She wanted to be brave and not upset Aunt Sharon any more than necessary. Even so, she couldn't hold the emotional pain inside any longer.

Captain Scott inched his way toward the bed. "It was a Cobra. Melody said he started the fire."

Sharon frowned. "A gang member! I'm so confused." She stopped and looked at Jordan. "Why didn't you and the captain know about the fire earlier? Didn't the firemen call your police units to respond?"

Jordan shook his head. "I'm sure they did. We were busy though."

"Doing what?" Sharon wanted to know.

"Rescuing me," Melody answered.

Sharon scratched her head and sat up straighter. "I'm really puzzled now. Can anyone explain things to me?"

Melody felt Jordan's hand land on her shoulder. She turned, looked at him and smiled faintly. She gazed back towards her aunt. "Right after Allen set our house on fire, he took me hostage and held me at gunpoint. It's a long story. There'll be time for details later. The thing is I'm safe now."

"Oh my, oh my, thank goodness, you're here now with us," Sharon exclaimed. "I've got a lot of blessings to be grateful for."

Sharon placed her hands over her chest and then grabbed her niece and hugged her so hard Melody's body hurt. When the embrace ended, Sharon leaned back and sighed. "Oh my, dear niece, I'm so sorry for everything. What are we going to do? Why, I lived in that house for fifty years."

Dr. Thompson interrupted. "You can stay here as long as you like, until you have somewhere to go."

"And I can go to a hotel," Melody said.

The doctor shook his head. "No, you can stay here for the night. I'll arrange to have a bed brought in here."

Jordan slowly brushed Sharon's tears away with the back of his thumb.

Seeing the gentle gesture reminded Melody how caring Jordan could be at times like this. He'd done the same thing for her when her father died. He'd lifted a thumb and tenderly wiped her tears away after the funeral.

Her chin shaking, Sharon cleared her voice, nodded firmly and gave a big sigh. "We'll rebuild, Melody. I've got savings." She looked at her niece. "I'm just glad you're still with us. Tell me exactly what happened to you."

Taking a deep breath, Melody began relaying everything that took place. When she finished, she placed a hand tenderly on Jordan's shoulder. "If it wasn't for Jordan and Captain Scott, I'd still be tied up under the bed…or worse…"

"I'm so thankful you're alive." Sharon glanced at Jordan. "And I'm so glad you were there for Melody."

Melody leaned over and gave her aunt a hug and kiss. Jordan rose from the bed.

Dr. Thompson grinned wide and took Sharon's blood pressure.

Sharon looked up at the doctor. "How am I doing?"

"Your pressure's up some, not bad under the circumstances. I'm going to prescribe a sedative for tonight. You've faced a lot today." The doctor stood up and turned to face everyone else. "All of you have."

Aunt Sharon nodded. "It's been a long day. I must admit I'm a little tired. Wish I could go home and sleep in my own bed though." Her eyebrows rose as a teasing smirk came to her face which Melody recognized so well. "I don't mean to complain, Doctor, but do you realize I hate lime gelatin?"

Everyone broke into laughter.

How did her aunt get everyone smiling again anyway? Melody wondered. She didn't know. Melody enjoyed the happiness. After Jordan laughed, he turned to Melody and winked.

Dr. Thompson grinned wide. "Mrs. O'Brien, I can't quite believe you're taking this so calmly. I'm pleased." He sat on the bed where Jordan sat earlier. "What's your secret?"

"Why, it's no secret at all." Sharon smiled. She flipped a partial bang from her forehead. "Look, everyone, I've lived through my dear husband's death."

"Right," Jordan informed the doctor. "He was killed in the same drug bust where Melody's father was killed."

The doctor nodded soberly. "Oh, yes. There's no doubt you've been through a lot of tragedy before."

Jordan took Melody's hand, gave it a quick squeeze and grinned. Her heart spun. Immediately, she reminded herself: Jordan wasn't flirting. He was only trying to cheer her up since she tragedy. The thought brought her back to reality. She reminded herself of what she needed to do. Regroup. How was she going to get the Cobras to leave her and her aunt alone? And what about Jordan? And everyone else? And where was Kim, her dear best friend? She would have to call her as soon as possible. She hoped, anyway, that Kim was okay....

After Jordan and Captain Scott left, Melody went to bed. She was exhausted. At least she was safe for the rest of the night. Melody didn't know what she would have done without her dear aunt. Here she'd moved to take care of her "second" mom she'd cherished over the years, and now Melody felt as if her aunt was caring for her.

Before she got to sleep, Sharon talked about the excitement of rebuilding her house. Her positive attitude rubbed off on Melody, who realized her aunt was being brave, showing her wonderful spirit. Melody figured she would start counting her blessings too.

Hours later, bright sunshine drifted through the hospital window. Melody woke. She could tell she wasn't fully rested. Even so, she was awake and couldn't get back to sleep. She decided to get up. She dressed, retrieved several magazines from a corner table and sat by her aunt's bed.

An hour later, her aunt woke up. "I'm afraid I fell asleep. How long have you been here?"

"Don't worry. I spent the night here. Remember?" Melody nodded to a bed in the same room.

"Yes, of course." Sharon straightened in her bed and attempted to fluff her pillow.

"Here, let me get that for you." Melody rose from her chair and flipped the pillow and helped her aunt get comfortable.

"You're spoiling me."

Melody smiled. "I see no problem."

Sharon laughed. "No, you wouldn't. How'd I ever get so lucky to be blessed with such a precious niece?"

"The same way I got so lucky to be blessed with you for an aunt." Melody laughed. "How're you feeling?"

"I'll probably be released today. I'm so happy."

"Where will we stay then?"

"We've got friends. The Hendricks already told me the two of us could stay there for as long as needed. They'd heard about the fire on the news."

Melody shook her head. "Some people are so nice. Warden Brewer said I don't have to come back to work right now either. He wants me to take it easy for the next few days.

"How thoughtful of him."

"Very. How would you like something to drink from the vending machine? I'm going to get myself something. A can of orange soda, perhaps?"

"No thanks. I must admit I'm still pretty tired."

"Go right back to sleep then. I'll be back in a moment."

"Okay, dear."

Melody slipped out of the room, went down the

hallway and reached the pop apparatus at the end of the hall. Just as she plopped her coins into the machine, someone slapped her back.

"Make one sound and you'll be sorry," a man's voice hissed in her ear.

Melody detected a dirty, oily odor from the guy's hand which covered her mouth. She wanted to ask what he wanted. His hand wrapped so tight around her lips, she couldn't even let out a squeal. She began gagging and felt the air escape her lungs. She struggled to breathe. Roughly, he shoved her to a nearby exit door and down several stairs.

"Now, I want to know where your boyfriend's at?" he snarled, breathing down her neck. He jammed his right shoulder into her chest. "Tell me."

"Boyfriend?" Melody asked weakly.

She didn't recognize the man. He probably was a member of the Cobra gang. At least, he certainly acted and sounded that way.

He pulled a shank from his pocket. *Another escapee?*

"Yeah, your boyfriend, Lakewater."

"He's not my boyfriend, and I don't know where he's at."

"Sure you do. Sonny sent me to get the info," the man said.

Melody saw the determination etched on his long, drawn face. If he was a prison escapee, Melody didn't recognize him, which wouldn't be out of the ordinary. She didn't know all the prison inmates.

She wanted to scream. She didn't for fear he would only stab her if she made a sound. With a quick karate move, she kicked the man in the groin and ran from him.

The guy's knife fell from his hand, and he fell down some steps. *Wack*! His head rammed into the cement wall.

Melody stopped, grabbed the knife and aimed the end point toward him.

The man slowly rose to his feet, gazed at her, and dropped his jaw, as though he couldn't believe what'd just happened. Blood poured from his nose and teeth. Melody raced up the steps, opened the exit door and let out an ear-piercing scream. The squeal was so deafening she surprised herself. In seconds, several hospital security guards were at her side, and a couple law enforcement officials handcuffed and hauled the guy off to the Pittsburg County jail.

Afterwards, Melody went back to her room to go to bed, after all the activity. She couldn't sleep. She sat by Aunt Sharon's bed. Her aunt fell back asleep, even through all the racket with Melody's scream and the ramblings of hospital security.

Melody thought of how fearful she'd been in Virginia over a couple nearby school shootings which took place when she was still teaching. And now here she was back in McAlester. Maybe she should have stayed in Virginia. At least then she wouldn't be facing all of the emotional turmoil from the tragedies: first the shooting and then the break-in at her aunt's home. Next the fire and Allen kidnapping her. And then, she recalled the fight a few moments ago with the Cobra. Oh, if only she'd stayed in Virginia, where she'd be safe! On the other hand, she wanted to help her dear aunt. Besides, if she hadn't come back to McAlester, she wouldn't have seen Jordan again. Now why did that mean so much to her?

She looked at her aunt, sleeping soundly. How she could sleep through the racket, Melody didn't know, but she was glad. Her aunt needed the rest.

Chapter 12

The next day, Wednesday, at the McAlester police station, Jordan's office phone rang. He picked up. "Hello, Lieutenant Lakewater, can I help you?"

There was silence.

"Hello. Who is this?" Jordan spoke again.

"Lieutenant Lakewater. I-I-I don't wanna give my name right now. Let's just say I'm at Big Mac."

Jordan jerked upright in his chair and tightened his grip on the phone handle. "You're calling me from prison?"

"Yeah. I gotta make this quick."

"I'm all ears."

"I heard you found the Tannehill trailer, but you didn't get Sonny and Allen."

"How'd you get the information?"

"Heard it through the grapevine here. It was on the news too. I heard somethin' else, info not on TV."

"Can you please identify the grapevine for me?"

"I can't. Sorry. I think I know where Sonny and Leo are at though."

"Where?" Jordan grabbed a nearby pen and notepad.

"In a cabin by Red Oak."

Jordan didn't say anything. That would have been the last place he suspected. Officials were covering the state. They'd mostly concentrated on Tulsa and nearby communities, since they knew a couple of Sonny's relatives lived in Tulsa.

"Can you give me the exact location?" Jordan gripped his pen.

"Yeah. I'll have to whisper."

Jordan pressed the phone closer to his ear. "Okay."

In seconds, Jordan jotted everything down. "We'll get right on it. Anything else you can tell me?"

"Yeah."

"What?"

"My buddy, I don't care to say his name, thinks Sonny and Allen have been selling drugs from the prison."

Jordan grinned. It wasn't the first time he heard about such cases, and those facts may help him and the captain on a potential drug bust they'd been working on for months now.

"Thanks a lot."

"And Lieutenant Lakewater, this buddy of mine…"

Jordan closed his eyes briefly and then pinched the top of his nose with one hand. "Yes?"

"He don't get on well with Sonny and Allen. He wants to take 'em both down, if you guys do find him and put him back here. My buddy wants me in on it. He says I gotta help. Man, I'm scared. I want outta trouble. I wanna get out of the slammer when my sentence's up. I'm almost there. Three months."

"Good thinking."

"And Lieutenant Lakewater…"

"Yes?"

"My buddy knows Tony McFarris is connected with Sonny and Allen big time. He's the guy who was just put in jail for the Wilburton robbery."

Jordan straightened in his chair. "Yes, I know who

Tony is."

Jordan gripped the cell so tight his fingertips turned white. It was hard for him to comprehend the guy was giving him so much information. Jordan hung onto every word. "I appreciate the information. Have you told the officials at the prison what you told me?"

"No, I don't trust the law enforcement."

Jordan frowned. "You trust me?"

"I heard you're a good guy."

"Where you'd hear that?"

The man snickered. "I saw you on TV in an interview several years ago. You sounded real nice."

Jordan shrugged. He didn't want to get sidetracked. Really, it didn't matter why the inmate trusted him. He now possessed material that he and the captain needed to act on.

The prisoner cleared his throat. "I want Sonny and Allen caught like you guys do. They're dangerous. One night in prison, they tried to stab me to death."

"I'm glad they didn't get the job done."

"Do ya' think the law enforcement could actually protect me from Sonny and Allen if they get back here?"

"Absolutely. Just give us your name."

He did.

Jordan grinned as he jotted the name on the top of his note sheet. "We'll do everything we can."

Jordan hung up and wasted no time to give the caption the information. Immediately, they held a briefing and, thirty minutes later, drove to Red Oak with a group of officers. During the next several hours, the search party frantically searched the cabin and talked to officials. No one found anything. Sonny and Allen were nowhere in sight.

****

Two days later, Dr. Thompson told Aunt Sharon he was releasing her from the hospital. The numerous tests he'd taken showed she didn't need surgery. Melody picked her aunt up and the two ladies spent the afternoon getting her settled in the Hendrick home where Melody'd been staying.

After evening dinner, Melody went up to the guest bedroom. She settled on a chair near the window. Sun shone on rain puddles in the front yard. Maple and oak leaves blew gently in the wind and sparkled in a vibrant green.

When Melody heard a tap at the door, she turned. Jordan stood in the doorway. He held a basket with a bouquet of yellow roses and white daises. Her breath caught at the thought of him giving her flowers. He often brought floral arrangements for her when they dated. Why would he do so now? Did he still have some feelings left for her? Feelings which could be reignited? She questioned if she was falling for the man all over again. She feared those kinds of emotions would make her life more confusing and complicated.

"Hi. The Hendricks told me to tap on the door. I hope that's okay."

"Of course."

"Is your aunt still sleeping?" he whispered.

She nodded.

He quietly strolled to Aunt Sharon's bedside and set the flowers on a nearby table. Then he rushed back to Melody.

"I thought she needed some spring flowers." He spoke in a soft voice.

Melody frowned.

"Well, I remember your aunt loves flowers," he began to explain.

"Oh, of, of course," Melody stammered, feeling foolish and embarrassed. How on earth could she have been so selfish to think the gift was for her? And why did it matter anyway?

He offered his hand. "How about we grab a cup of coffee at the Lazy Lounge? The Hendricks said it'd be no problem. While you're gone, they'll keep an eye on your aunt."

She wrapped her fingers around his palm and welcomed the warmth of his skin, sending wonderful vibrations through her. "Sounds great. I love the place. It's usually quiet there."

"My thoughts exactly."

He led her into the hallway.

Suddenly, she remembered she never combed her hair. She ran one hand through her curls. "Oh no, I haven't combed this mess. I must be some sight!"

Jordan grinned wide and eyed her up and down. "Yes, you're one attractive lady."

She looked at him and sheepishly smiled. "Will you give me a moment to run a brush through my tangles?"

"Sure."

Moments later, at Lazy Lounge, Melody strolled to a corner table and took a seat.

Jordan sat across from her. "How are you doing? Alexandria told me everything, including how you were the one responsible for getting a Cobra arrested. Congrats. I'm just sorry I couldn't have been there."

"Nonsense. You can't be in two places at one time. You need some rest too from your injuries. I never did find out if you were even able to get much sleep the past weekend. I know you were busy Monday and Tuesday. How well I know!"

He chuckled. "I got tons of sleep last weekend, probably thanks to my pain pills."

"Great."

"Please excuse me. I'll get our coffees."

"Sure."

Getting up, Jordan purchased two coffees from a vending machine, grabbed two packets of dry creamer and placed the items on their table.

He sat down. "Still double on the cream?"

"Humn?"

"Do you still take cream in your coffee?"

"Oh, yes, thanks." Why couldn't she think around this man? She took the packets, opened them and poured the contents into her cup.

"How are you doing, after everything?" He took a sip of coffee.

"Okay, I guess. I'm still quite shaken from everything." She stirred her coffee.

"Quite normal, under the circumstances."

She sighed.

"What's wrong?" he asked.

Melody shook her head. "I experienced a real meltdown after the Cobra was arrested."

She never meant to bother Jordan with the emotions tumbling in her the past couple days. He'd always been so easy to talk to, and she felt fear rising in her. Was she still in danger?

His dark eyes widened, and she saw his concern for her.

"Tell me about it." He took another sip of coffee.

She forgot how comfortable he could make her feel.

She began telling him everything, to get if off her chest, afraid of not being able to function if she didn't learn how to relax again.

She concluded by saying, "On top of everything, I'm feeling guilty about Tim Barlow's death. He died late last night, you know."

"Yes, I heard."

"If I never shot him—"

"If you hadn't shot him, you'd be dead."

Melody knew his words were true. Still, mixed feelings stirred in her mind.

Jordan cleared his throat. "I don't think you realize how much turmoil you've been through. It takes a long time to deal with such a situation. You remember how I felt after I killed a man during the drug bust?"

Embarrassed, Melody drew a quick breath. "Do you mean the drug bust with my father?"

Jordan nodded.

"You didn't have a choice. You shot the drug dealer to save your life." She shook her head. "Jordan, I'm sorry. At the time, I grieved so much over my father. I didn't think much about what you were going through after you killed one of the drug dealers. How dreadful for you."

When he took her hands, she melted inside.

"It was terribly hard and yet, at the same time, I felt so bad about your father dying. If you only knew what happened—" He stopped abruptly.

Melody frowned. "What happened? Is there something about the raid I don't know?"

She could see it was as though she'd sent a bolt of electricity through him. He let her hands drop to the table.

He shook his head vigorously. "Nothing, forget it. I shouldn't have brought it up. I apologize."

Exactly what happened during the drug bust? She wanted to ask, but from his pale face, he looked like he'd been through enough shock for one day.

Afterwards, the conversation wasn't the same.

Chapter 13

Later, Jordan took Melody back to the Hendricks' home. Two days passed without much activity. Melody decided she couldn't take it any longer. She needed something to occupy her mind, get her thoughts off danger, if possible. Going back to her prison work would be hard to face, but she needed to do it sometime, and she figured the sooner the better. She'd go this afternoon if the captain allowed it. After a quick telephone call to him, she was on her way.

The Hendricks kindly let her use their minivan since the Cobras smashed her vehicle.

"Good morning," Warden Brewer said, when Melody entered his office. "How are you?"

"I'm okay, considering everything."

The gray haired man got up from his desk and gave Melody a hug. She welcomed the embrace. She'd always liked the warden. He was a good man and wonderful to work for.

After the hug, he took a couple steps backward and frowned. "Are you sure you don't want some more time off?"

She shook her head. "I've got to do something today, or I'll go crazy thinking about everything."

Warden Brewer gave a nod. "I understand. We're glad to have you back." He escorted Melody through the prison rotunda. "You're one brave person. The prison will be forever grateful."

Melody waved her hand. "You're like everyone else, giving me too much credit."

The warden laughed. "You're so much like your father."

Melody took the statement as a great compliment.

They passed the storage room where she'd been held hostage. Her heart beat harder. She flung a shaky hand to her forehead. She became dizzy and her mind flashed back to the riot...She remembered how terrified everyone was...how tension hung in the air...how time seemed to stop when she'd pulled the trigger...how horrified Tim Barlow looked when she shot him...how loud he crashed on the floor...how sick she felt to her stomach...She'd replayed the nightmare over and over in her mind.

The warden gazed at her. "You okay?"

She nodded weakly. "Yeah. Returning to the scene of the crime proved more difficult than I envisioned though. Reality's setting in. I'm going to have to pass by that room every day." She nodded toward the door.

"You can still go home if you're not up to this."

She shook her head vigorously. "I've got to face this sometime. If I go home, I'll just worry over the weekend. I've got to see my office again, work there and get comfortable in such a setting again."

Warden Brewer gave her a couple pats on the back. "I completely understand."

She looked at the warden and smiled. "Thanks for escorting me inside."

He grinned and placed a hand on her shoulder. "No problem. We're a family here. You can count on us. I'll be happy to walk you back to your office every day if it makes you feel better."

Tearing up, she glanced his way. "How can I ever thank you?"

Gently, he released his hand from the upper joint of her arm and patted her hand. "No thanks needed. Remember we're here for you."

She entered her office with the warden. She used to love coming into the room and smelling the freshly waxed floor. She'd have a cup of coffee and study her case files. She always said she would never have a job which was in any way connected with danger. Sometimes, though, circumstances change things. Since the school didn't have any job openings when she moved back to McAlester, she was grateful Kim knew about the case manager opening.

Kim. Where was she? Melody still didn't know.

The warden began to go out the door.

"Warden…do you have a moment?"

He turned to face her. "Yes, hon, what is it?"

"Have you heard from Kim? I'm terribly worried. I tried to get hold of her, ever since the riot, and she's not returning my calls."

"Oh, she's fine."

"I'm thrilled to hear! Why didn't anyone tell me?"

He scratched his cheek. "I'm sorry. Everything happened so fast around here—"

"I'm just glad she's okay," Melody interrupted. "Is she at work now?"

"No. She won't be coming in today."

"Everything's all right. Isn't it? She didn't get hurt in the riot; did she?" Melody bit her lip.

The warden sighed and closed the door. "No, not at all."

"What is it then?"

"Please don't worry. She won't be coming in for a few days. I'm not sure when she'll be back."

"What's going on?" Melody frowned.

She wasn't certain, but she actually thought the warden turned pale for a few seconds.

He shook his head. "She's been busy and asked for some time off."

Melody felt her shoulders lighten. At least she didn't have to worry about Kim anymore. Or she didn't think so.

"Kim's safe. Isn't she?"

The warden coughed. "Yes. She lost one of the inmates she was assigned to in the riot though. I'm afraid she's taking it quite hard."

"I didn't know. I'll call her when I get off work."

Mr. Brewer held up his hands. "Please, don't."

Melody shrugged her shoulders. "Why not?"

"She's going through a lot of grief right now." The warden rubbed his hand through his hair. He stopped for a second, folded his hands and shook his head. "Eight people now have died from the riot."

Melody took a deep breath. "I'm so sorry. I'm afraid I made it a point to not listen to the news the last couple days. I got tired of hearing it."

"Quite understandable."

"When can I call Kim?"

The warden frowned and spread out his hands. "Why don't you wait until she comes back to work? I think she just wants to get some rest."

"Oh...okay." Melody spoke in a weak tone. Why didn't the warden not want her to call her dearest friend this evening?

For the first time, Melody stopped to realize she was blessed she didn't have any of the inmates she worked with killed in the tragedy. It was hard enough knowing people, both prison officials and inmates, were shot to death, and she killed one of them. She still didn't know how to deal with the situation.

The warden placed his hands on his hips. "Listen, inmate Ron McGraw wants to see you. I almost forgot to tell you. I have no idea what he wants to talk about. He wouldn't tell me. As you know, he's not easy to deal with. Would you mind talking to him now?"

"Not at all."

"If he gives you trouble—"

"After the riot happenings, I should be able to handle him," Melody interrupted.

Warden Brewer grinned. "You've got more confidence in yourself than you realize."

She smiled. "Maybe so. I already feel good about coming back this afternoon. Then I'll have a weekend break, and Monday I'll won't be so fearful of coming back to work."

"You're reminding me of your father again. Remember though I'm just a buzz away if you need anything."

"Sure, thanks. Oh, wait a moment." She dashed to the coffee area, in the corner of the room, and began making a pot of coffee. "I'm making my go-go juice. Want a cup before you leave?"

"No thanks. If you're going to be okay, I better get back to my office. As you can imagine, I've been swamped with work since the riot. We have a 23-hour lock down now."

"I'd heard, and I think it's wonderful. Our new

environment should really help us."

The warden nodded. "Yeah. This was the shortest riot, in terms of time, in the prison's history and one of the most destructive."

After the warden left, Melody locked her office door and began some paper work. She surprised herself. She actually focused on getting some things organized, more so than ever.

Thirty minutes later, she heard a tap on the door. She shoved her papers aside to clear her desk. She strolled to the door and unlocked it. Inmate Ron stood with an officer.

The officer nodded to Melody. "Let me know when you're finished."

"I will. Thanks."

"Good afternoon, come in." Melody nodded to Ron.

He entered and the officer left the two of them alone.

Melody pointed to a chair. "Have a seat, please. How are you today?"

He grunted and sat down.

"I understand you wanted to talk to me." Melody sat in the high-backed chair behind her desk. "What can I help you with?"

Ron snickered, folded his arms, and sat back on the chair until only two of the stainless feet set on the floor. "Help me? I'm here to help you."

Melody raised her eyebrows. "What's up?"

He leaned forward, sending the chair back on all fours. "What do you want to know?"

Melody took a deep breath. "I want to know everything on your mind."

Ron began talking, giving details about the riot. Melody jotted everything down on her computer screen.

So far he didn't say anything yet that she already didn't know.

Suddenly he stopped and coughed several times. He cleared his throat. "I don't quite know how to tell you this part."

"What part?" Melody asked.

"Well…"

"Just tell me. Officials here will want to know everything. We have to get Sonny and Allen captured, or no one will be able to rest."

Ron's dark eyes widened as he nodded his head. "Ain't that the truth of it."

"So, what is it?"

"One day, by mistake, I got hold of a message kite meant for Sonny. It was from Leo."

"Do you still have it?"

Ron shook his head. "Wish I did, but I flushed the thing down the toilet."

"What did it say?"

"Sonny, Allen and Leo were planning to make a bomb."

"An explosive?" Melody cringed. "What for?"

Ron shrugged. "Dunno. All the note said was, 'Remember, we've got to get materials for the bomb as soon as we get out.' There was nothing else in the note, except it was signed by Sonny."

"Get out? Of where? The prison? Were they planning to escape? Were they the ones who planned the riot?"

Ron scratched his head of dark hair. "Yeah, at least the rest of us think so."

"Did you ever hear any of the other inmates say anything about a weapon?"

"No, never did."

"Well, this is big information. I'll definitely tell the authorities. Thanks." She titled her head and studied him. "I'm curious about something though."

He cracked his knuckles. "Oh yeah? What?"

She gave a half-smile and a half-frown at the same time. "Is it my imagination, or are you going to cooperate with us?"

He hung his head, gave a heavy sigh and then slowly looked up and grinned. "It's not your imagination, ma'am. You killed one of the big Cobras. Some of us, like me, who's not part of the gang, are grateful. Tim Barlow was a real trouble maker, and one of the gang's big boys. Always fightin' with someone. With him gone, maybe the Cobras won't harass the rest of us so much now. Especially me."

Melody nodded. "Good."

After the session, Melody went to the warden and told him what Ron told her.

Mr. Brewer shook his head. "You remind me so much of your father. You certainly got a lot of information. We've got work to do. Lots of it. I don't want to scare you—"

Melody fumbled with her pink neck scarf. "What?"

The warden sighed. "Perhaps I shouldn't say anything. I don't want my imagination to run away."

"Isn't that part of your job? We've got to think of every angle."

The warden shrugged. "You're right. I was just wondering what Sonny and Allen want with a bomb. Who or what do they plan to destroy?"

Melody nodded. "Good question. I don't know."

Mr. Brewer leaned forward. "I'll get to work on it.

Let me know if you think of any place or anyone Sonny, Allen and Leo might want to terminate."

"Sure."

Six hours later, Melody was anxious to go back to Hendrick's home. She'd been on edge ever since hearing about the bomb. She packed her papers, wormed her way through the rotunda and got clearance for the three gates to open. As they snapped shut, she realized she was looking forward to a calm evening more than she could say. If such a thing was possible, of course.

Outside, birds chirped in the air. Golden leaves fell gently to the ground. The day was perfect for a picnic supper, but such a thing was out of the question. She didn't want anyone, except the police, of course, to know where she was living since the fire.

She got into the car, started the engine, eased out of her prison parking space and slowly drove onto a nearby street. Traffic was light.

Moments passed.

Just when she neared Hendrick's home, she felt something bump into the back bumper. Oh no! She glanced out her rear view mirror to see a tan Honda. She couldn't see the faces of the driver or passenger. Perhaps it was Sonny and Allen. Biting her lip, she was determined not to let the situation get the best of her. She wanted to keep her cool. To her surprise, the vehicle passed her. Did the driver bump into her accidentally? Or on purpose?

Instead of getting back onto the main Carl Albert Highway, she took a turn, drove down several blocks and pulled onto a cement parking lot of a new fast-food place, Mad Dash. She parked and retrieved her cell from her purse. Who should she call? She didn't have time to vacillate. She remembered when they were at the hospital, Jordan made her promise she would call him if she needed anything. He even offered to drive her to and from work today. She'd refused. Now, she was sorry. She punched Jordan's contact number.

Someone tapped her car window. She jolted and turned to see a food server. Holding the cell phone in one hand, she rolled down the car window.

He smiled. "Can I help you?"

"Sorry. I didn't see you. I'll have a Diet Pepsi, please."

"Can I interest you in a hamburger and fries today, ma'am?"

"No, thanks anyway."

"Okay, be back in a jiffy."

Just then she heard a voice on her cell, "Hello, this is Lieutenant Lakewater."

Quickly she rolled her window back up.

"Jordan, this is Melody."

"You sound upset. What's wrong?"

"You were right."

"About what?"

She sighed. "I should have let you take me to work today."

"What happened?"

She took a deep breath and gave him the details. "Could you send someone over to follow me home? Just to play it safe?"

She heard him take a long sigh. "I wish you'd let me take you to work today."

She tapped a finger on the steering wheel. He sounded angry, and she couldn't blame him. The last thing she wanted was for him to be disgusted with her.

"Where are you?"

She could tell he tried to speak in a controlled voice. "Mad Dash, the new fast food place."

"Are you in danger now?"

"No, at least I don't think so. I'm afraid things could go there fast. I don't know if the car bumped me on purpose or if it was an accident."

"How long was the guy been on your tail?"

"I'm not sure."

"What do you mean? You don't know how long he followed you? Why aren't you being more aware of what's around you?"

She heard the sharp edge in his voice.

He took a deep sigh. "Boy, I wish you would have let me take you to work today."

"I wanted to prove myself. I wanted to do things on my own."

"You already proved that at the riot. There comes a time when you need to rely on others for help."

"I know. You were right. Okay? I really don't need a lecture right now. I'm already scared. What if the two guys in the car were Sonny and Allen?"

"Try to relax. I already sent an officer your way. He should be there shortly. I'm afraid I can't pick you up myself, because I'm swamped with work today."

Was he really busy with work? Or was he mad at her?

Chapter 14

Melody stared at her phone. Jordan'd hung up abruptly without saying good bye. He never did that before, not even when they were dating. Did she really do such a bad thing?

She bit her lip so hard it bled. She hoped she wouldn't see the tan car again and an officer would come soon. She nervously tapped her polished fingers on the steering wheel. She didn't want to wait much longer before an officer escorted her home.

Tap, tap, tap.

She jumped.

"Your order?" The carhop spoke loud in order for her to hear.

Melody jerked to attention, as she yanked down her window. She'd forgotten about the soda pop she ordered. She reached into her purse, got some coins, gave them to him and took the soda.

"Thanks."

"You're welcome."

She started to roll up her window, then remembered she'd forgotten a tip.

"Wait a minute." She set the Styrofoam cup of pop in the car container and then reached into her purse, retrieved a couple dollars and plopped them into his hand. "Here's a tip for you."

"Thanks a lot."

"Uh hum." Melody nodded, biting her lip.

"Ma'am?"

She glanced at the guy. "Yes?"

"Are you okay?"

"Sure, of course, I'm fine. Why?"

"Your hands were trembling when I handed you your drink."

"I have trouble with low blood sugar."

Well, it wasn't exactly a lie. Even so, Melody knew she wasn't having trouble with hypoglycemia now. Her problem was fear. She'd developed a migraine over the past few moments at the thought of the tan Honda and who could be driving it.

The food server grinned. "My mother has low-blood sugar. You know the diet soda isn't going to give you any sugar. How about an ice-cream cone also?"

"No, thanks anyway. I need to get home fast."

He frowned. "Are you sure? It'll take me just a minute."

"Positive."

"Very well then. Have a great day." The guy left and trailed back inside.

Melody rolled up the window.

Still shaking, she took a sip of soda. She wanted to get a grip on her nerves. Setting the liquid back in the car container, she glanced out her rearview mirror, hoping at any second to see a police officer. Why wasn't anyone coming? Had something bad happened?

Just then a couple officers pulled into the entrance of Mad Dash and parked across from her. She nodded to the men. They didn't glance her way. Instead, the driver turned off the engine and rolled down his window. He punched the red button to order and then glanced at his partner.

What on earth was going on? Why would they be placing an order, instead of driving to where she was so they could follow her home?

She kept staring at the policemen. She waved at them. They didn't notice. Or at least they didn't seem to. Perhaps they knew she was there. Maybe they were playing it safe and had a plan. Whatever, she would wait as long as it took. She took a deep breath to relax.

She turned her focus back and forth from the policemen to the rear view mirror. Nothing happened. Jordan must have sent the policemen.

Glancing at the guys again, Melody saw the carhop come out with two Styrofoam cups. He handed the containers to the driver, who took them and handed one to the other officer. The motorist rolled up his window and set his Styrofoam cup down. He started the engine and slowly eased out of the parking space.

Terrific. Melody was relieved. She started Hendrick's vehicle, but when the policeman came around the other end of Mad Dash, they drove by her and onto the highway. She rolled down her window.

"Wait!" She waved at them. Again, they didn't notice. She rubbed her hands on her pants and kept her eyes on the officers, now disappearing into the traffic. What should she do now? Obviously, Jordan never sent these men. Was help still headed her way? She turned off the engine.

Just then the Honda, she'd seen earlier, swung into Mad Dash and pulled into a parking space near her. A second later, the driver of the vehicle, a young man with reddish-brown hair, nodded at her and grinned. He yanked down the car window and plopped his arm on the door edge. On his hand was a Cobra tattoo.

Her heart leaped to her throat. Her mouth became dry. She wanted to take a drink of her soda to help her relax. She knew she didn't dare though. Her hands shook furiously. She needed to get out of here. Fast. If only there was time. It was too late.

Besides, where would she go? The Cobra would no doubt follow her.

How on earth was she going to protect herself now? She couldn't. Still grinning, the guy kept staring at her. She glanced away and pretended like she never saw him. She heard his loud laugh, filled with ridicule, intimidation, victory.

Quickly, an old, black, Buick, sedan pulled between her and the Cobra. Her breath caught. The man turned his back to her as he apparently studied the other guy.

Melody wondered if the two men knew each other. Were they planning something?

Just then the Cobra backed up, yanked out of the driveway and into the traffic.

The man, in the other car, turned toward Melody.

Relief poured through her as she recognized Bill Zimmerman, who'd been a dear friend and co-worker of her father. Bill nodded and smiled at Melody, then pulled his car out of the driveway and backed up, giving her space to pull out in front of him.

She did.

If Bill was in uniform, the Cobra might have shot him, Melody realized. And her.

She drove from the parkway and began going home with Bill following close behind. Then it occurred to her. She needed to call Jordan back. Right away. Her father taught her to never talk on the cell phone when she was driving, unless it was an emergency. Well, this was a crisis she needed to report. She reached for her purse with one hand, zipped it open and retrieved her cell. She punched Jordan's contact again.

"Lieutenant Lakewater."

"Jordan, I'm sorry to—"

"Bill Zimmerman came to get you," he interrupted.

"Yes, I'm on my way back to the Hendricks'. Bill's following me."

"Good."

She noted concern in Jordan's voice. Did he actually care what happened to her? Or was he angry with her for not allowing him to escort her home as he'd wanted to do?

"The tan Honda came again and parked by me. It was a Cobra. I saw the gang tattoo on his hand."

"We're on it, dear. Bill called and gave me the license number. Don't worry. We've got plenty of information and already have a couple guys to get this Cobra too."

"Fantastic. I'm so relieved."

Melody noted Jordan called her dear…

Moments later, Melody and Bill arrived at Hendrick's home.

Inside, everyone hugged everyone.

Aunt Sharon frowned. "Why didn't you call us? You were supposed to have been here some time ago."

"I'm sorry. I'm really not so late though."

"Is everything okay?" her aunt wanted to know.

"Everything's fine now." Melody decided she wouldn't add any details, let Bill give the information, if he wanted.

"Bill!" Aunt Sharon raised her hands to her cheeks.

"With all the commotion, I just recognized who you are! I can't believe it. Bill Zimmerman, how are you? And how's your dear wife?"

Bill nodded soberly. "She passed on a little over a few months ago."

Aunt Sharon frowned. "The cancer?"

Bill nodded yes.

"I'm so sorry."

"Thank you. If anyone knows what it's like to lose a devoted spouse, it would be you. You know how fond I was of your husband."

"Yes, I certainly do. And he thought the world of you too."

Bill cleared his throat. "I'm so sorry Melody has to be in the middle of all this. Don't worry about her though. The police have her protection as number one on their priority list. Don't worry."

Mr. Hendrick nodded. "We're glad to hear that."

Bill scratched the back of his gray hair. "Someone was trying to follow Melody here."

"I'm afraid it was a Cobra," she confessed.

"Oh no!" Aunt Sharon flipped her hands to her mouth.

Bill looked at Sharon. "Don't worry. They will get the guy. I'm certain. I got his license plate. You know how Jordan's right on the ball. He's got a team out there right now to track the guy down. I wouldn't be surprised if he's already been caught."

Melody sighed. "I should have let Jordan follow me home like he'd wanted to do. Stubborn me. I wanted to be independent."

Bill gave Melody a quick hug. "I'm just glad you're safe now. Be careful until we get everything back to normal."

Aunt Sharon grabbed her niece's hand for a few seconds and then released it. "Yes. I'm so glad you're okay."

Mrs. Hendricks smiled at Melody. "We've been thinking of you, dear."

Melody kissed her aunt's cheek and turned to Mrs. Hendricks. "I appreciate it."

Bill nodded to Melody. "I've got to run. Jordan will be in contact with you later today. He said to be sure to tell you."

Immediately, Melody noted a sly smile spread across her aunt's face. "Now, Aunt Sharon, don't go making a big deal out of Jordan wanting to see me. It's an investigation, police business."

Her aunt's eyebrows rose. "What? Me? Make a big deal?"

"Yes, you." Melody chuckled.

"I'm just glad Jordan's coming over. I've got some of those delicious chocolate chip cookies you made from my recipe the other day." She turned to Bill and winked. "Why, once Jordan tastes those cookies, it's hard telling what will happen. The way to a man's heart is through is stomach, you know."

"So I've heard." Bill grinned.

"Auntie!"

Aunt Sharon's eyes widened. "I didn't say anything."

Melody held up her hands. "You didn't have to. One of your smirks is worth a thousand words. Besides, you seem to forget, we're not living in our own home."

Mrs. Hendrick's waved a hand. "Don't be silly. Jordan's more than welcome to come over anytime."

Aunt Sharon smiled. "Thank you, dear. I knew you wouldn't mind."

Bill laughed. "Sharon, you haven't changed. You're still great at match making, I see."

Even though she'd been so terrified only moments earlier, Melody smiled at the way the conversation slowly drifted to laughter.

After a few moments, Bill said, "Well, folks, I've got to go."

Aunt Sharon folded her hands in front of her and swayed back. "Aw, why don't you sit down for a visit? It's been years, Bill."

"What a great idea," Mrs. Hendrick said. "In fact, why don't you join us for dinner? I've got a roast beef in the oven."

Bill sniffed the air. "Is that what smells so wonderful?"

Mr. Hendrick nodded. "Yes. Join us. It'll be fun."

"I'd love to, but I'm still on duty."

"So, when can you see us again?" Sharon wanted to know.

Bill grinned. "I tell you what. I'll make it a point to come over sometime soon, so we can catch up."

"Wonderful!" Mrs. Hendrick's said.

Sharon unfolded her hands and straightened. "That's fantastic, Bill. I'll look forward to it."

Bill dashed out the door.

Chapter 15

A couple hours later, on the front porch of the Hendrick home, the sight of Melody took Jordan off guard. How could she look so good every time he saw her? She wore red slacks and a matching silk blouse. A tiny stone sparkled on a necklace at the base of her throat. He wanted to take her in his arms and kiss her, confess she was igniting all kinds of feelings in him, feelings only a man could have over a woman he cared about.

But now wasn't the time. Or place. Would there ever be a time and place? He stopped. *Get your mind on the business at hand.*

"Melody, I need to talk to you in private."

"Sure, let's go upstairs to the bedroom lounge."

They climbed the green, carpeted stairs to the room which was her temporary home now.

Each sat in an oversized, stuffed, gold chair by the window. He let out a slow breath. He still wasn't ready for the lecture he was about to give her.

He raked a hand through his hair, rubbed his hands on his slacks and cleared his throat. "I don't know how to begin."

"Maybe I can make things easier. I know you're upset with me, and you've got every right to be. I should have let you take me to work today."

"Well, I'm glad you came to your senses."

She took a deep sigh. "Okay, I know you're furious

126

with me. I'm sorry. Just say whatever else you have to say and get it over with." The tears began spilling down her cheeks. "I don't know why I'm too stubborn for my own good sometimes."

Jordan rose from his chair and wiped the tears from her eyes with the back of his thumbs. Her skin was soft to his touch and pleasurable. "I've always attributed part of your personality to Aunt Sharon."

"You'll forgive me then?" She spoke in a soft voice.

He knelt in front of her and took her hands. "Of course. I care about you. You've got to understand. I was afraid for you, and I didn't want you to get hurt."

Jordan noted how warm her skin felt. He lowered his head, kissed her hand and returned to his chair.

Melody sighed. "I know. You were only trying to protect me, not control me."

"Dear, I'd never want to control you. Why can't you trust me?"

He'd called her dear again. Why couldn't he be sensible and talk normal around the woman?

She looked at him. "To be frank, I think it's because I dated a man in Virginia who kept telling me what to do. If I didn't succumb to his orders, he'd get furious. Thankfully, we broke up. I thought Max was the man for me. When he started seeing someone else, I knew he wasn't like you. I trusted him, only to find out later he was going out with another girl."

The thought of another man hurting her emotionally hit him in the gut. "I'm sorry you faced that type of thing."

He never knew Melody dated anyone. He took some women out after their break up, or at least he tried to. After escorting a few women to various events, he realized the females seemed too engaged in themselves, living a high-society lifestyle. After a while, he figured he'd never find the right lady for himself. Sure, he wanted to settle down someday with a wife. And he'd always wanted to be a father. He loved children. He tried not to think about the dream these days. It hurt too much.

Melody's eyes widened. "My relationship with Max would have never worked. I thought he was like you. He wasn't at all."

Now why did those words please him so much? Did he still have a chance with her? No, of course not. She made that clear when she left to go to Virginia.

Besides, he couldn't tell her, not now, maybe never: he was responsible for her father's death. The truth was nearly more than he could bear…He stopped thinking about the past any further. To relive the scene again would only weigh him down, and he didn't need the extra stress.

He refocused on Melody. "Promise me something though."

"Name it."

"You'll let me take you to work until we catch the Cobras in McAlester."

"Yes, I promise."

"Thank you, Melody, dear."

He said dear again. He couldn't help himself. She could melt his heart in an instant. With a wide grin, he rose from the chair and eased Melody to her feet and then to his chest. They stood together. He felt the heat from her radiate to his body. Business or not, he desired to find out how she felt about him. Now. He couldn't take it any longer. As he spread his hands across her back, he closed his eyes and drew her near to him. More than anything, he wanted to know if she still experienced any feelings for him, like he felt for her now. He felt her minty breath as he neared toward her. He welcomed what he would be feeling in only a second, his warm lips over hers.

There was a knock at the door. "Hot chocolate."

He jumped at the interruption and laughed. "I love your aunt, but sometimes her timing is way off base."

Melody smiled. "Tell me about it."

She opened the door.

Steam rose from three hot cups of chocolate, setting on a tray Sharon held. "Let me set this down."

Aunt Sharon set the platter on the desk. She retrieved a cup, held it in her hand and started out the door. "Enjoy."

Jordan raised his eyebrows. "You don't want to stay?"

She turned and grinned. "Not really. I know when I'm not needed."

Before either of them could say anything, she closed the door.

Even though they were alone again, Jordan refrained from taking Melody back in his arms. He wanted to, but Melody held two cups of chocolate.

She handed a mug to him. "Here you go."

Well, Jordan thought in dismay, she apparently didn't want the kiss nearly as bad as he did. He might as well forget her and any possible future they may have together. Still, how could he be near her and not express his feelings?

Jordan noted how pretty she looked with the lamp light spreading across her red hair. He shook his head to come to his senses and refocus.

"Now, Melody, de—"

"Yes?"

"We have to talk."

"About what?"

He wanted to say "about us" but instead he got to business. "About the bomb. The captain told me about it."

She recoiled. "Yes. I want to tell you everything and help in any way possible."

"Great." He realized he'd be able to see her again, at least until the investigation was over.

"What do you want to know?"

Jerking to attention at Melody's question, Jordan began asking her about the situation. Melody did not hesitate to answer all his questions in exquisite detail.

An hour later, pleased with Melody's cooperation in giving him all the facts she knew about the bomb, he left and headed for home. A question lingered in his mind: She was willing to help him with the investigation, but would she consider exploring the feelings he carried in his heart for her?

Chapter 16

Three hours later, in middle of the night, Melody woke up startled. She thought she heard something. She crept out of bed, dashed to the window and slowly opened the drapes a couple inches to see what was going on. Was someone in the backyard behind the rose bushes? Heart racing, she surveyed the area. Yes, a man knelt to the rear of the flower hedges. Who was he? The Cobras wouldn't know she lived at the Hendrick home now. Or would they?

A cold chill went down her spine.

The guy snapped a flashlight on and held it towards her. She ducked out of sight and crept to the bathroom. There she peeked out of the tiny window, and this time she saw two men behind the bushes. She recognized both: Sonny and Allen!

In seconds, she raced to her cell phone, called 911 and told the operator everything. Then she called Jordan. She needed to talk to him, tell him what was going on, so she could calm down. He was great for helping her that way.

"Hello," he answered.

"I hate to bother you this time of night—"

"What is it?"

"I saw Sonny and Allen in our back yard."

"Oh no! I'm calling 911 now."

"I've already called. They've contacted the police,

and Sonny and Allen already took off from the yard, jumped in a car and sped off. Hopefully, they'll be caught shortly."

"I'm coming over. I'm going to protect you. We're going to catch these guys before they can hurt you or anyone else anymore. I give you my word."

Melody couldn't say why, but the information coming from him eased her more than she cared to admit. She didn't want to develop more fondness for the man. It was going to be hard enough to tell Jordan good-bye after the investigation was over, and she wouldn't be seeing him on a regular basis.

"Thanks. I owe you, big time."

"Not really." He chuckled. "You saved my life. Remember? Now, I want you to try to wake everyone as calmly as you can. I'm putting everyone in the protection witness program. We're not taking any more chances."

"Oh no! We have to leave here?"

"Do you have any better suggestions?"

She sighed. "I guess not."

Jordan cleared his throat. "I'm getting in the car now. I want you to stay on the phone with me. First wake everyone up."

"Okay."

To Melody's surprise, everyone took the information much better than she'd hoped for.

Everyone dressed, packed some clothing and other essentials and met in the living room to wait for Jordan.

Moments later, when the doorbell rang, Melody answered. Moonlight beams shone on Jordan. Only moments ago, she'd been fearful for her life and now, seeing him, she felt as though she didn't have a care in the world. Now, why could one man send those highly magnetic and warm kinds of sensations to her?

"Come in."

He stepped inside, and she closed the door.

"As you can see, we're packed and ready to go." Melody looked down at the red robe she wore. "Oh my, I packed, but I forgot to dress! I didn't put on one thing."

Jordan laughed lightly. "Well, you didn't exactly take anything off either."

In the midst of the drama, Aunt Sharon and the Hendricks laughed. Which was so like Jordan, Melody realized. He was a lot like her aunt; he could bring out the laughter in everyone in the midst of a crisis.

"I'll be just a second." She dashed from the living room and raced up the stairs.

There, she shivered as she remembered how only moments ago Sonny and Allen stood in the yard. Shaking her head, she raced back down the stairs and into the living room.

"Jordan, I just thought of something!" She heard the panic in her own voice.

He raised his eyebrows. "What?"

"Don't you want to send the police after Sonny and Allen?"

"I already called the locals, and you said you just called 911."

Melody slapped her forehead. "How did I forget?"

"It's easier than you think when you're panicky in the midst of a situation."

Pacing back and forth, Melody twisted her hands together. "Only moments ago Sonny and Allen were in our yard! Where do you suppose they're headed?"

"Don't know. The law enforcement is out in full swing." Jordan walked into her personal space and took her hands. "Hon, you did the right things. Now we need to let the police handle the situation and get you and everyone in this house to safety."

Sharon looked at her niece. "He's right. Better run upstairs and get dressed quickly."

Melody glanced at her aunt and then Jordan as she gently pulled her hands from him.

She dashed up the stairs, slung off her robe and slipped into a pair of slacks and a blouse.

Moments later, outside, everyone piled into Jordan's car, and they were on their way. It took about an hour for them to get to the house where they'd be staying. The home was located in an addition near Henrietta.

Jordan eased into the driveway.

"Do you think we'll be safe here?" Sharon asked Jordan.

"This is as secure as you can get. My men have this home surrounded. And your next door neighbor to the right is an undercover cop. No one knows, so make sure not to say anything."

"Sure, we'll play it safe," Mr. Hendrick responded.

"Yes, it's the least we can do," his wife added.

About twenty minutes later, everyone settled inside.

Melody shrugged and frowned. "What about my work? What am I going to do?" Why didn't she think of that before now?

"Don't worry. We don't want anything to look suspicious. You'll be going to work as usual. We don't want the inmates to think you're hiding out somewhere, and you're afraid."

Melody twisted her hands together. "How will I get to and from my job?"

Grinning, Jordan bowed. "Meet your new chauffeur.

I'll be driving you."

Melody smiled. "Thanks."

How she admired Jordan. Every day he faced potential danger. Regardless, he never lost his sense of humor or courage. How did he do it? He reminded her so much of her father. He'd always been that way, and, no doubt, Melody realized, police and law enforcement officials took things in stride all the time. They needed to in order to survive. She truly admired them and the way they protected the citizens of their community. She felt Jordan's protection now, and it was more comforting than she could explain.

He appeared tired, and she could certainly understand why.

Mrs. Hendrick smiled. "I noticed we have groceries and everything. Would you like a cup of coffee before you head back to McAlester?"

"I'd love some, although I'm not going back to McAlester."

Melody frowned. "Where are you spending the night?"

"Here." He grinned. "I want to make sure everyone's safe."

Her aunt smiled at her.

It wasn't because Melody didn't want him there. She did, with all her heart. Even so, she needed to give him assurance they would be okay.

She looked at him. "We'll be fine. You said we're well protected."

"Now, let's not interfere with the man's life." Sharon helped Mrs. Henrick get the makings for coffee. "We can make a bed for him on the sofa."

"Actually, there's five bedrooms in this house. So,

I'll be able to sleep in one."

"Even better." Sharon kept smiling.

Melody crossed her arms. "Don't you need to be back in McAlester? Aren't you worried about Sonny and Allen?"

"Of course I am, which is why I want to stay here. I'm worried about all of you too. Everyone in the police force is looking for the two Cobras, and the captain said I needed a good rest tonight to keep healing my injuries. Besides, this way I can take you back and forth to work."

Riding back to McAlester on work days with Jordan wouldn't be so bad, Melody thought. In fact, it sounded safe, secure, and…even nice.

Later, in the bedroom, Melody brushed her hair. There was a gentle knock at the door. Automatically, she jumped. Then she realized probably no one dangerous stood on the other side of the door. She was in a safe community now.

"It's Jordan. May I come in?" His voice was soft, husky and masculine.

She opened the door. "Of course. What do you want?"

She didn't know if it was her imagination, or if Jordan looked slightly embarrassed.

Chapter 17

Jordan thought about Melody's question. *What do I want?*

He sighed. If the truth be known, he wanted to take her in his arms, hold her tight and kiss her. He longed to sweep his hands through her soft hair and tell her not to worry, and she didn't need to be afraid, that nothing bad would ever happen to her again. He couldn't say those things though. No one could predict anyone's future. And, he wasn't about to deceive her, like he'd done so long ago.

If she knew his actions in the drug bust killed her father, she wouldn't want to be in the same building with him. Would he ever be able to tell her the truth about her "papa" as she used to call him? The ache he felt to tell Melody everything and get it off his chest was almost more than he could bear. He feared he had to keep silent on the subject. The last thing he wanted was for the woman to walk out of his life.

Suddenly, it struck him. He couldn't deny his feelings anymore, even if it was only to himself. He was falling in love with her all over again.

Tilting her head, Melody narrowed her eyes. "Well?"

He cleared his throat and hesitated.

She opened the door wide. "I've never seen you at a loss for words. Come in."

He entered. "I'm here to double check the windows, make sure they're locked."

When he said the words out loud, he wanted to kick himself. What would the woman think? That he thought she was helpless? Melody was a strong woman. She could stand her own with the best of them. And she'd saved his life. How was he ever going to repay her?

She smiled. "I already checked them, but feel free to take another look."

Inspecting the windows, Jordan noted every one latched securely. So why didn't he want to leave?

For a moment, there was an awkward silence. He unbuttoned the top button of his shirt. "I'd better be going. Don't worry. You'll be safe here."

He saw relief escape from her eyes. He needed to protect Melody until officials caught Sonny and Allen. Or else, he'd never forgive himself. It was the least he could do.

He studied her. Her wide green eyes captured his heart. What would it be like to kiss her again? On the lips? To feel her soft body caress against him? Wasn't it worth a try?

He shifted his weight, wondering how to proceed next. He couldn't afford to mess this up. His heart would break all over again if she refused the kiss he was about to give her. On the other hand, he heard a warning voice inside his head, telling him that he should stop now, back out before it's too late. Play it safe all the way. Keep his feelings to himself. Leave Melody alone.

He didn't listen to the voice. He already waited too long. His body cried out for her to wrap her warm, long arms around him and feel her tender mouth on his. Did she want him as much as he wanted her? Did she have any feelings for him at all, besides a general friendship? Or weren't they even friends?

Slowly, he moved toward her and took a wisp of her hair between his fingers and then gently slide the strands behind her delicate ear. Her warm, vanilla breath sent a stimulating sensation through his stomach. His fingers and arms tingled. He leaned over and softly kissed her forehead. Memories raced in his mind, thoughts of the love they'd once shared. Was it possible to reignite the flame they carried in their hearts so long ago? And if so, how?

He closed his eyelids halfway as pleasure kept flooding his insides. A soft groan escaped him. He could stop now, not kiss her. She took a step closer to him, her body now brushed his chest as she entered his personal space. She closed her eyes.

"Jordan," she whispered.

That was the green light he needed. A slight tremor developed in his hands from the high frequency of vibrations pouring through his body. With one sudden move, he ascended on her soft lips. At first, he feared she'd pull away, because her body tensed. Then he heard her give an inward, short, sigh as his lips met hers, and she wrapped her arms around him.

Her mouth stimulated him beyond belief. The kiss was full, warm, intoxicating, making his motions rise to a height which scared him. She'd made it clear she'd never marry a policeman. He pulled back and opened his eyes.

Melody frowned. "Did I do something to displease you?"

Displease him? If the situation wasn't so serious, he would have laughed. The last thing the woman could do was dissatisfy him, even if she tried.

"No, of course not. The kiss should never have happened. I'm sorry. Trust me. I won't let it happen again. I'll deal with my feelings like a man from now on. You won't have to worry about anything."

****

Melody's heart fell in dismay. The last thing she wanted to hear was he'd never kiss her again. The enduring gesture felt so warm, so loving. She needed to get over the intense feelings, which burst into a flame at the touch of his lips. She couldn't afford to fall in love with Jordan again, only to realize they could never be husband and wife. A life like that would never work out.

No doubt Jordan already figured that part out too.

No doubt that was for the best.

She reminded herself that he was in constant danger every day. He never knew what would happen. The job he loved presented serious potential consequences. Why did she have to fall in love with a policeman in the first place? She knew why. Because Jordan was a loving, caring man with high morals, a tremendous personality and a great reputation. He'd make a great husband and father one day to one lucky woman. Unfortunately, Melody knew the woman wouldn't be her.

She could never marry a law enforcement officer. Or could she? Was she changing her thoughts? After all, working at a prison, she too faced danger….

The week end flew by without much happening. Melody, Aunt Sharon and Mrs. Hendrick cleaned and sanitized the apartment, since it'd been empty for several months. Jordan and Mr. Hendrick mowed the lawn and fixed a leaked, water pipe. As for Sonny and Allen, they remained at large while the law enforcement units combed the streets of McAlester and the state of Oklahoma.

Monday morning sunshine burst through a tiny crack in the yellow kitchen curtains. When Jordan walked in, Melody did a double take. How handsome he looked. He wore a white, knit shirt and a pair of well-pressed, navy blue slacks.

She nodded at him. "Are you working undercover this morning?"

"Yeah, afraid so. Can't take any chances with Sonny and Allen. Who knows where they could be? Some authorities think they may have left the state."

Melody frowned. "And you don't?"

Jordan took a deep sigh. "Not necessarily. Regardless, we'll still keep looking."

"Of course."

Sharon, standing nearby, flipped some potatoes over in a frying pan. "Melody made a great breakfast."

"Looks good." Jordan sniffed. "Smells good too."

Melody smiled. "I've got a cheese omelet with diced ham, mushrooms and green pepper here and biscuits in the oven. They're almost done."

"I hope you're hungry, son," Sharon said.

"Starving." He kissed Sharon on the cheek.

Melody studied Jordan's face. All she could think about was the kiss they'd shared Friday night. Did the gesture mean as much to him as her? No, she immediately answered herself. Somehow, someway, she needed to find a way to get the man out of her heart. Oh yes, she admitted it to herself over the weekend. She'd fallen in love with the guy again. Or, perhaps, she never fell out of love with him. Whatever, she needed to forget him. After the kiss, he made it obvious there was no future for the two of them.

"Sleep well?" She attempted some small talk.

"Yeah."

She didn't say anything further, but she barely got any sleep. She rolled, tossed and turned all night thinking about the man…and the kiss… and the fact he no longer wanted her. Could she blame him? Not really. When she turned down his proposal, she certainly didn't expect the guy to wait for her to see if she changed her mind. Life wasn't fair. She got it. She needed to move on. She just didn't know how.

After breakfast, she rode in Jordan's undercover vehicle, his personal, silver Toyota, to go to work.

He glanced her way. "I never asked you. How was your shuteye this weekend?"

Was he attempting small conversation too? Or was he really concerned about if she'd got a good rest?

"Not very well, I'm afraid."

His eyebrows swirled high. "Were you worried?"

She nodded yes.

"Remember what I said?" He took her hand and gave it a quick squeeze and then placed his hand back on the steering wheel.

"No, I'm sorry, I don't. What'd you say?"

"I'd keep you safe."

She nodded.

He frowned. "You don't seem convinced."

Tears came to her eyes. "I'm sorry. After the riot and everything…I'm constantly on guard, always looking over my shoulder to see if anyone's there."

"Things will get better. They always do."

"I hope so."

Suddenly, a car from behind them hit their bumper

and gave a jolt.

"Oh no!" Melody exclaimed.

"Hold on! There's a guy behind me, and I think he's trying to cut us off. I've been watching him for a while now, and he's slowly gained speed. I've got to get the man. He's either one crazy dude who doesn't know what he's doing, or he's someone we want arrested."

"Do you think it's a Cobra?"

"Maybe."

She raised her eyebrows. "Sonny or Allen?"

"Maybe."

She shivered at the thought.

Suddenly the driver of the yellow Ford entered the other lane. He pushed Jordan's vehicle to the side of the road. The Toyota bounced and jolted. The rough ride made Melody's stomach tense. She glanced at the other vehicle. She got a good look at the driver.

"Oh no!" she exclaimed.

"What is it?"

"He has a large Cobra tattoo on his arm."

"You sure?"

"Positive."

"We'll catch him. I'm calling for backup now. Since we're still near Henryetta, the police here can set up a roadblock. Hold on. I'm going to inch over his way and try to push him in front of me."

Chapter 18

Jordan didn't want to put more drama in Melody's life, but with the Cobra near them, he couldn't afford to let the guy get away. He yanked the car into full gear and began accelerating at a fast speed. Out of the corner of his eye, he saw Melody bite her nails.

He glanced her way. "Everything will be over in just a few minutes."

He wanted to say everything would be fine, but how could he? Both of their lives were at stake now. Double danger.

He grabbed his cell phone and punched the contact for the nearest police department.

"How can I help you?" a policeman answered.

"This is Lieutenant Lakewater from McAlester, and I'm driving southbound one mile from Henryetta. I need road blocks set up right away."

"What's happening?"

In seconds Jordan gave him the information.

"We're on it," the officer said.

With sweaty palms, Jordan set his cell phone on the dashboard. He gripped the steering wheel. "I'm afraid the drive is going to be a little hectic. Traffic's heavy."

Cars honked, and the drivers changed lanes at intervals on state highway 75.

Melody said, "At least we're not heading towards Tulsa. It looks like most of the traffic is going that way."

"True." Jordan noticed Melody's positivity in a negative situation. She was so like her father.

He knew he needed to do something quick to catch up with the guy who bumped into them. The driver was several cars ahead of him. Jordan pulled out his portable siren, rolled down the window and plopped the device on top of the car.

He snapped the siren on full blast. "Sorry. It looks like you're in for a wild ride again."

Melody gave a nervous chuckle. "No problem. I just want the guy caught."

"Better snap off your seat belt and get on the floor again. You're probably getting used to this by now."

She immediately heeded to his orders.

As the siren kept roaring, cars pulled to the side of the road to give him the right of way. Jordan speeded ahead and, seconds later, caught up with the guy. He signaled for him to pull over.

Instead of the man slowing down, he raced ahead of Jordan. Seconds later, the SUV hit the ditch. Steam rose from the engine.

Jordan yanked to the right and pulled to the side of the road.

He glanced down at Melody, still curled on the floor. "You okay?"

She nodded, her hands wrapped tightly across her stomach. "Yeah."

"You can get up now. I'm going to make me one arrest."

Jumping out of the car, Jordan raced to the guy, still seated in the passenger's seat. "Can you explain why you were going so fast, young man?"

The guy snarled, "I wasn't."

"Right. Ninety-five miles per hour isn't high-speed, and I'm Little Red Riding Hood. Let me see your driver's license, please."

The man clenched his teeth and hissed under his breath. "Good grief!"

He retrieved his license from the glove compartment and handed the document to Jordan.

Taking the license, Jordan read the guy's name and other statistics: Name: Greg Salvers; height: 6'3"; weight: 170 pounds.

After he jotted the information down, Jordan gave the card back to Greg. "Step out of the car for me, please." He knew Greg Salvers was a Cobra and possibly shared connections with Sonny and Allen.

Greg stumbled out.

"Place your hands on the vehicle, please."

"Why?"

"Just do as I say."

Instead of obeying Jordan, Greg ran to a nearby, barbed-wire fence, stretched his long legs across the wire and zoomed across pasture land.

Jordan raced to the fence and climbed over it. His injured arm stung with pain. Ignoring the discomfort, he ran until he caught Greg and knocked him to the ground. He swung a leg on top of Greg's body and grabbed a set of handcuffs, hanging from his uniform. With one quick move, Jordan snapped the metal rings around Greg's hands and pulled him to his feet.

Greg frowned. "What're you arresting me for?"

"Speeding. I've also got a question, a great big one."

"What?"

"Where are Sonny and Allen?"

"Sonny and Allen who?"

Jordan raised his voice. "Don't play games with me. I'm going to get the information whether it's from you or someone else. I see you're a Cobra."

Greg's face turned ashen, and his lips trembled.

Jordan gripped Greg's arm. "So where are your two friends? Start talking!"

"I don't know."

"So you do know them?"

Slowly, Greg shook his head. "Every Cobra knows them."

"So where did they go?"

Greg tipped his head and then let it flip forward. "Why don't you talk to Leo? I bet he knows."

"We already did a couple times. He said he doesn't have a clue where Sonny and Allen went."

Greg snickered. "Aw, come on. He knows. He just doesn't want to snitch."

Jordan realized his next move was a no-brainer. He would take Greg to the police station and then interrogate Leo at the prison again.

An hour later, at the prison, the warden arranged for another interrogation.

In the interrogation room, fluorescent lights shone bright. Leo sat at the narrow end of the table. Jordan and Captain Scott stood at the other end.

"I hope you level with us today." Captain Scott paced from one end of the table to the other.

Leo grunted and said nothing.

The captain stopped pacing, pulled a chair in front of Leo and sat down. "Come on. If you know where the two gang leaders are or even where you think they may be, you'd better tell us."

Leo squirmed in his chair. "Hey ya'll, you can just

stop right there."

Jordan took a seat. "Actually, we can't. You're an accomplice to a murder, which makes you eligible for a very long term in federal prison, if we can't find Sonny and Allen."

Leo's hands trembled.

Captain Scott crossed his arms. "We're trying to help you. We've got to find them."

Leo shook his head. "I know nothing."

The captain looked at Jordan. "Looks like he's still the only one going down for the murders then."

Shaking his head, Jordan gave a low whistle. "Yeah, too bad."

Leo's eyebrows rose as he cracked his knuckles. "What do ya'll mean? Why're you houndin' me like this? What do 'ya want from me?"

Captain Scott leaned forward. "For starters, we can't find your bros, at the moment. Now where are they hiding?"

"How would I know? I can't keep track of them when I'm cooped up in this (blankety blank) hole." Leo's face turned red, and he let out a slew of more profanity.

Captain Scott slammed his hand on the table as he rose from his chair. "Look, don't get smart with us. This isn't our first barbecue. It might be your last though."

Leo's nostrils flared. He glanced up at the captain. "What do you mean? Is that a threat or something?"

"It means you will be sorry if you don't cooperate with us." Jordan leaned back in his chair.

Leo jumped to his feet. "Hey, I ain't stupid. Sonny and Leo don't call me Brains for nothin'. I've got one, 'ya know."

"Then use it!" Captain Scott raked a hand through

his hair. "Sit down, and start talking now. You can't be as innocent as you're trying to make out."

Jordan held his hands behind his back. "Yeah, start answering our questions."

Captain Scott cleared his throat. "Did Sonny and Allen ever mention anything about making a bomb to you?"

Leo's blue eyes widened. "A bomb? Hey, I know nothin' about no bomb."

"Then tell us where Sonny and Allen are staying." Captain Scott sighed.

"Give us the information now." Jordan pulled a chair in front of Leo. "And you'd better tell us everything this time."

Leo flopped back in his wooden chair, hung his head and twisted his hands.

Jordan looked at Leo. "Do you really want to be the one charged for these murders?"

The inmate glared at Jordan. "I already told you where Sonny and Leo were."

The captain nodded. "Yes, you did. In fact, the directions you gave us were right on. Only problem is Sonny and Allen weren't home when we got to the trailer. They'd left. So where are they now?"

Snapping his knuckles, Leo hung his head. "Why should I tell you?"

"So you avoid getting in more trouble," Jordan said.

The captain deepened his voice. "Yeah, so you don't get a longer prison sentence."

Leo blinked rapidly, tightened his shoulders and raised his hands. "All right! All right! Sonny and Leo may be holdin' out in a cabin near Red Oak. I ain't sure though."

"We need directions on how to get there." Jordan leaned forward.

To Jordan's surprise, Leo gave them.

Captain Scott and Jordan looked at each other and grinned.

The interrogation was over, at least for now, Jordan realized. The next thing on the agenda was to get to Red Oak. As soon as possible.

Moments later, in the conference room, computer printed maps of the rural Red Oak community were spread across a long table. Captain Scott stood with the other officers, bending over the charts.

He cleared his throat. "Now, gentlemen, listen up. I called you for this meeting because we just got a tip from inmate Leo. Sonny and Allen may be hanging out in a location near Red Oak. Take a look at the route I've charted."

"Red Oak? Why there?" one guy questioned.

Jordan shook his head. "We don't know. You never know what dangerous guys like these are going to do. They move around a lot to keep from being caught."

Wasting no time, Captain Scott pointed out different places on the map as he gave the policemen assignments, planned for the capture if they found Sonny and Allen. "Gentlemen, study this particular chart I enlarged. We want to be there as soon as possible to make sure we don't miss anything. To capture these guys is going to take a lot of hard work and precision. Hopefully, we'll catch Sonny and Leo this time. Does anyone have any questions?"

There was silence.

He nodded to the men. "Good. Now we will give appropriate weapons to carry. I delegated extra men to be on duty. As you know, some officials thought Sonny and Allen may have left the state. Now we think it's probably not likely. Remember, the Cobras destroyed millions of dollars' worth of equipment in the riot and left us with eight fatalities. These inmates won't stop at anything. Cobras are noted for being extremely dangerous, the worst kind of criminals we have here, so again I'm warning you that everyone needs to take extra caution, so no one gets hurt."

"Yeah," several officers agreed at the same time.

"Let's gooooo now," the captain roared.

Minutes later, the men wore their weapons and marched out the door.

Nearly an hour later, outside, in the country, the air was still and muggy with the humidity in the eighties. Captain Scott slowly drove toward the edge of a heavily wooded area, stopped, turned off the engine and picked up his binoculars. After he surveyed his surroundings, he nodded and grinned at Jordan. The captain handed him the field glasses.

Jordan looked through the lenses and yelled, "Bingo! Looks like it's the cabin."

"Yeah, I'm radioing the other officers."

In a moment's notice, about a dozen men surrounded the rustic, log house.

Jordan knocked on the door. "Open up! Police!"

No answer.

"Police! Open the door now!" the captain shouted.

Silence.

In seconds, several officers bolted inside with the captain and Jordan.

The living room featured an overstuffed, brown, leather sofa and two recliners. A large black-and-red rug covered most of the dilapidated, hardwood floor. A couple open bags of chips and several empty beer bottles set on a coffee table.

Quickly, the officers went from room to room and then back to the living room.

Jordan slapped his hands on his waist. "Looks like no one's here."

One officer nodded. "Yeah, apparently someone's been here though, and I got a feeling it was Sonny and Allen."

The others nodded in agreement.

Jordan looked at the captain.

Captain Scott put his hands on his hips and glanced at everyone. "I suspect Sonny and Allen were here and left in a hurry. Keep scrounging the area, both inside and outside. Search the cabin well to see if you can find any papers or anything which could give a clue to their whereabouts." He stopped and looked at Jordan. "I was able to get the names of the couple who own the cabin. I want you to come with me, and we'll question them. Perhaps they know something."

Jordan flashed a grin. "Good idea."

The captain and Jordan went outside, while the rest of the working force stayed behind to carry out the captain's orders.

"Be safe," the captain said, walking out the door.

Outside, Jordan and Captain Scott got in the police car and sped off.

Fifteen minutes later, they drove near a white house, surrounded by red, purple and gold flowers.

The captain nodded Jordan's way. "I think it's the place. I'm going to back out of the trees and see if we can't move onto the country road. I'm afraid if our car pops up suddenly from this forest, we could scare Mrs. Anderson, who gets frightened easily and forgets things. That's what I was told anyway.

"Better play it safe, even if it will take a little longer."

About ten minutes later, Captain Scott pulled onto the country road. "Shouldn't be long now."

"Right. I think, according to the map, we'll be going about six miles out of our way, since we're back on country road."

"Yeah, backing out of these woods really slowed us down. Man, it's rough terrain."

Jordan glanced at a computer printed map. "I'll say. My stomach feels every hilly spot we drove over."

Captain Scott laughed. "A complaint?"

"Not at all. You drove through this madness a lot better than I could have." Jordan grinned.

"Thanks. I'm just glad we still have some sunlight. It'll be getting dark soon."

Five minutes later, they pulled up in front of the home. A German shepherd raced to the car and barked.

"I hope someone's here." Captain Scott held his chin high.

"Me too."

Jordan and the captain stepped out of the car. Jordan looked at the dog and held out a hand. "Down, buddy, down boy. We're not going to hurt you."

The dog turned, ran to the front door and barked. Jordan and Captain Scott followed the animal up the three, wooden porch steps. A white cat sat on the edge of the porch railing.

Jordan knocked on the door.

Seconds later, a man came to the entrance. He

nodded with a friendly smile. "Gentlemen! Anything wrong?"

"We hope not," Jordan answered. "Are you Mr. Brian Anderson?"

The man ran a hand through his gray hair and wiped his palms on his worn, blue jeans. "Yes. What can I do fer' ya?"

A woman came to the door and stood by the man. She frowned. "What's happening, dear?"

Brian put his arm around the petite lady. "Don't worry." He looked at the captain and Jordan. "This here's my wife, Karen."

The captain nodded and grinned at the woman. "It's nice to meet you. We just have a couple questions, shouldn't take long. We're with the McAlester police force."

Jordan pulled a couple of mug shots of Sonny and Allen from his folder and showed them the pictures. "We want to know if you have you seen these guys anywhere?" He handed them the glossies and pointed to one. "This is Sonny Furemore." He paused and pointed to the other photo. "And this is Allen Shiver."

"We heard they might be in the area," the captain explained. "They're escaped inmates from McAlester."

The lady flipped her hands to her face. "It's our new renters!"

Brian stiffened his posture. "Yes. They came to our place yesterday and asked if we'd be willing to rent our cabin for the weekend."

Karen stepped closer to examine the photos. "At least I'm pretty sure that's them."

The captain radioed the officers, searching by the cabin, and gave them the information. Before he hung up, he gave a warning, "They're probably somewhere in the area. Be there shortly. We're getting more information from the land owners, the Andersons."

Karen opened the door wide. "Come on in, officers and have a seat. We'll tell you everything we know."

"Thanks." Jordan nodded.

Inside, she pointed to a large, stuffed, red sofa. A matching red, shag carpet covered the floor. "I'm glad I just vacuumed."

Brian chuckled, "Hon, I keep telling you the house doesn't have to be spic and span for everyone who comes through the door."

Jordon settled on the sofa. The captain joined Jordan, while Brian settled in a large, black recliner.

Brian scooted forward. "How can we help?"

His wife stood by him. She frowned. "I suspected those two were up to something all along."

Jumping up from the chair, Brian rushed to his wife and kissed her check. "Don't be alarmed, dear. We'll handle whatever we need to, just like we've been doing for the past forty-six years of our marriage."

Weakly, Karen nodded as her husband put his arm around her and led her to a small matching love seat, sitting opposite the sofa. They both sat down.

"I hope we can settle things." Tears came to Karen's hazel eyes. She looked at Jordan and then at Captain Scott.

"First, what suspicions did you have about the two guys?" Jordan asked.

Taking her husband's hand, Karen looked at Captain Scott and Jordan. "When they showed up here to rent the place for a weekend, I told Brian I didn't like the looks of them."

Jordan frowned. "Oh, why?"

Letting go of her husband's hands, she shrugged. "Both have a tattoo of a coiled snake. Now there's nothing wrong with tattoos, mind you. I mean I'm not prejudiced or anything. It's just that tattoos gave me the creeps."

"It's the Cobra gang sign," Jordan said.

"Right." Captain Scott nodded.

"Oh, dear!" Karen exclaimed.

Captain Scott shook his head. "Do you have any idea where they went now?"

Brian shook his head. "None whatsoever. I can tell you one thing though. I must have just missed them yesterday. I was at the cabin to check on things. To see how they were getting along and if they needed anything, like towels and stuff. When I got there, no one was home, but they had been. They couldn't have been gone long at all."

"Why do you say that?" Jordan raised his eyebrows.

Karen nudged Brian's elbow. "Tell them what you saw."

Brian gave his wife a quick smile and then looked at the captain and Jordan. "When I got inside, there were two fried pork chops in a frying pan in the kitchen. The meat was still warm. I couldn't figure out why anyone would leave in such a manner."

"Must have been in a big hurry." Captain Scott rubbed his hands together and leaned forward.

"They probably wanted to hide quick. They're in a lot of trouble," Jordan said.

Brian sucked in a quick breath. "Yeah, a great big hurry. Why, steam was coming from the chops and everything. I took off to see if I could find them." He paused and shook his head. "I didn't see nothin'. I'm sorry I didn't contact the police. I didn't know they were in a gang. I gave them the benefit of a doubt. They gave us a long sad story about them being homeless for a while and finally got jobs."

"They were obviously lying," Jordan said.

"Yeah, these guys are really dangerous Cobras. They're two escapees from the prison riot. Didn't you see their pictures on the television?" the captain inquired.

Karen shook her head. "I'm afraid not. Our television's broke and neither of us watch much TV, so it's been out of order for about two months now." She took her husband's hand and patted it. "I'm just thankful, hon, you're here, and you didn't get hurt."

Brian frowned and looked at the police. "I'm not in trouble. Am I? I mean it wasn't against the law to rent to them or anything. Was it?"

"No, you're not in trouble. You didn't have any way of knowing they were criminals. The information you gave us is useful. Now what kind of vehicle did they have?"

Karen shrugged and opened her hands. "That's another thing which puzzled me. They just walked up to our place."

Jordan glanced at her husband. "Seriously?"

Brian nodded. "My wife's right. When we asked them about not having a vehicle, they explained they were hitchhiking."

Jordan rubbed his hands together. "Do you have an idea where they could have gone?"

Mr. Anderson shook his head. "I'm afraid not. There's not much around here, except us quiet country folk. I should have listened to my wife. I never should have rented the place to those two. I figured it was just an old cabin which my great-great uncle lived in and is in such terrible shape now anyway. Figured I might as well make some money on it, before I tore it down. Besides, they paid in advance, and we needed the money. Seemed to have a lot of cash on themselves."

"So, you were planning to get rid of the cabin?"

Karen smiled. "Yes, my hubby's been wanting to get rid of the residence for several years. It has interfered with our peanut crop time and time again."

Brian looked at Jordan. "Where do you think the renters could be headed?"

Jordan shrugged. "Boy, we'd love to know. I will say this. It's not unusual for gang members to have several different locations where they live."

Karen frowned. "Why?"

"To leave quickly before the police find them," Captain Scott explained.

"Then it looks like Sonny and Allen got what they wanted." Karen spoke softly.

"Yeah." Jordan sighed.

"My wife does all the bookkeeping around here. Would you like to look at her records?"

Karen nodded. "A lot of times I jot little details down. My thoughts. May not have nothing to do with business. I do remember writing down some things I thought about Sonny and Allen."

Brian looked at Jordan and the captain. "Maybe the two of you can find out some detail, something which could help us track them down by looking at my wife's notes."

"Sure, we'd love to take look at those records." Jordan ran a hand through his hair.

Karen rose from the sofa. "Follow me."
The captain and Jordan rose to their feet.

Chapter 19

Later, at the prison, Melody sat behind her desk. She glanced at her watch: 4:45 p.m. It was nearly time to go home. Jordan said he'd take her back to the witness protection home where they stayed last night.

Her phone rang. She stretched over a pile of paperwork to reach the handle. She picked up.

"Hello."

"Hi, it's Jordan. You doing okay?"

She raised her eyebrows. "Yes. What about you? I called earlier to see if you still planned to take me back home after work, or do I need to find someone to get a ride?"

"No."

Her heart skipped a beat at the thought of seeing him again. "You'll be here shortly then?"

"Hold on. I got your text. What I mean is I've already arranged for your transportation."

"Oh?" The information disappointed her.

Even though she figured they wouldn't ever have a future, she still enjoyed being with him. She actually longed for the guy.

In a moment, he gave her the details and then ended the call by saying, "Gotta run. Warden Brewer and I have been busy, and the job's not over by any means. We're still hunting for Sonny and Allen. Promise to call if you hear anything from your end."

She gripped the phone tighter. "Certainly."

"If I don't make it back tonight, don't worry. Have no idea how long this is gonna take. I just hope they can be captured tonight."

Her hands became clammy. She gripped the phone tighter. "Any luck so far?"

"Nothing I can say over the phone."

She wanted to say she was thinking of him and sending warm thoughts his way, but he'd already hung up. Was he angry with her over something she did? Or did he really have to hurry? Even if he needed to hustle, couldn't he have at least said one simple word: good-bye?

By the time a coworker escorted her back home, she still didn't have the answers.

Several hours later, in the living room of the witness protection house, Melody curled in the recliner and tucked her feet underneath her. She picked up a magazine to relax while everyone else already retired early for the night. After flipping through some pages, she decided to call Kim. She couldn't stop thinking about her friend. They never spoke since the riot, over a week ago. Kim never came to work yet either and, with each passing day, Melody worried more about her.

Maybe now Kim would be willing to talk. Melody would have called the warden to clear things with him, before she made the call, to make sure it'd be okay to call her friend, but he was busy. Besides, he could say no. She decided to call anyway. The abrupt call with Jordan upset her more than she cared to admit, and perhaps a phone visit with her friend would cheer her up a little. Besides, hopefully, she could help Kim too, in some way, with her grief. She'd do anything for her best friend.

Pulling her cell from the pocket of her long, pink robe, she punched Kim's contact number. Kim's cell phone rang three times. Melody held her breath. Was Kim going to answer or not? She waited for another ring to leave another message.

Just then Kim's voice came over the phone. "Hello."

Melody's jaw dropped. "Kim! Are you all right?"

Kim hesitated. "Yes."

"Why haven't you answered my messages I left on your phone? I've been worried sick about you!"

"I told Warden Brewer I wanted to be left alone for a few days. You know one of my inmates died."

"Yes, the warden told me. I got so tired of waiting to hear from you. Warden Brewer said you'd call when you felt like it. I hope you don't mind I called tonight."

"It's okay." Kim's voice sounded shallow, not like herself at all. "I haven't been myself lately. I should have called."

"What's going on?"

"Nothing."

Melody knew Kim answered much too quickly. She decided the warden, Jordon and her friend must know something she didn't. Melody became more concerned. Why was everyone being so secretive with her?

"How are you dealing with your inmate's death?" Melody cleared her throat and continued. "He's the one you were pretty close to. Right?"

"Yes. He was really working hard in the rehabilitation program. He reminded me of my brother so much before he died of the drug overdose. I was so proud of inmate Mason for getting off the drugs. He came from a home life next to unbelievable and pulled himself out of the terrible mess."

"I'm sure you played a big part in helping him."

Kim sighed. "I don't know about that."

"Do you know why he got involved in the riot?"

Kim gave a few sobs. "He didn't. Another inmate roared into his prison cell and stabbed him in the back sixteen times."

"Oh, how terrible! What can I do for you?"

"I should be asking you the same question. I heard about your courage."

"I wasn't as brave as you think."

"Yes, you were. You're a real heroine. The situation could have been so much worse if you hadn't killed Ted. He was terribly dangerous."

"I just wish he never died. I'm having such a hard time dealing with the fact I actually killed a man."

"It will take time to adjust. You've been in my thoughts."

"Thank you." Melody realized she shot a man, and no one, not even her best friend, gave her a hard time over it, like she feared people may do. Kim was always there for her. She longed to talk to her more about the shootings. She felt a conversation with her friend would help sort her feelings to deal with the future. "I'd love to sit down with you and have a heart to heart talk. You've made me feel better already. Can we have coffee or perhaps lunch tomorrow?"

"I'm afraid not. Jordan and I are meeting—" Kim stopped abruptly.

Melody nearly dropped the phone. "Jordan?"

Kim quickly replied, "Forget I said it. I wasn't supposed to say anything."

"Why not?"

"Nothing."

"Are you seeing him?"

"Not really."

"What then?" Melody couldn't stop with the questions.

"Forget it. You'll find out soon enough."

"Find out what?"

"Don't give it another thought. I'll tell you all about it later."

Melody's heart pounded, and she broke into a sweat. Why was she so upset? Jordan and Kim could see each other. Both of them were single, and she turned down Jordan's proposal long ago.

Kim continued. "With the aftermath of the riot, it's been hard. We'll have a long talk as soon as I get back to work."

"When?"

"I have no idea at this point. Warden Brewer said you went back to work Friday afternoon. How did things go?"

"Okay, except I was followed home by a Cobra."

"How awful for you! Didn't you have someone escort you home from the prison?"

"No, Jordan offered. Like a fool, I said no."

"Oh, he did?"

Kim sounded puzzled.

There was a long pause, and then Kim said, "I imagine it was quite hard to see Jordan again."

Melody nervously picked up a nearby pencil and rolled it over and over between her fingers. "Actually, yes. I tried to deny my feelings at first…"

She stopped.

Melody said more than she planned. She didn't want

Kim to know she experienced feelings now for a man she could never have. Especially not after Kim said she planned to meet Jordan.

"It's hard I'm sure," Kim was saying. "I'm sorry you have to go through dealing with all of those feelings, especially right after the shootings."

The words were nearly more than Melody could bear. Tears filled her eyes. She was on the verge of bursting into tears. She bit her lips to refrain.

Kim cleared her throat. "I'd better get off the phone. Warden Brewer wants me to keep my line as free as possible."

"Why?"

She heard Kim sigh. "I'm talking too much. We'll have coffee as soon as I get back to work."

"You just said you didn't know when."

"True. I promise we'll get back together soon though."

"Bye," was all Melody said.

She didn't know if she wanted to see Kim again. If Jordan and Kim were an item these days, Melody wasn't sure she could remain friends with Kim. Or Jordan.

The next morning, Melody, Aunt Sharon and the Hendrick's sat at the breakfast table.

Ashley Hendrick frowned. "I'm so worried about Jordan."

"I'm sure we all are." Sharon looked at Melody. "Have you heard anything else?"

Melody sighed. "Not other than they're still searching for Sonny and Allen."

Mike Hendrick took a bite of eggs and a sip of coffee. "The news said they still haven't found the two escapees."

"Do you think Jordan's in danger?" Ashley Hendrick's eyebrows rose.

Sharon nodded her head and looked at Ashley. "Honey, after being married to a policeman, I realize police are in danger every day of their lives." She took a sip of coffee. "You just learn to live with it and send warm thoughts their way."

Melody glanced at her aunt. She'd never heard her aunt express such strong emotions about the police before. If only she could be more like her relative, accept the fact that law enforcement careers are risky. Yet wasn't that what she was learning to do these days by working at the prison? She began to feel like she could be a policeman's wife someday. What good did those thoughts do her now, after what Kim said about planning to meet the man today?

Jordan and Kim. She couldn't get the two out of her head.

Sharon took a sip of coffee and looked Melody's way. "What time's Bill coming to drive you back to McAlester to take you to work?"

"He should be here any minute." Melody smiled at her aunt. "Do I detect a little anxiousness to see him again? I noticed you dressed especially nice today."

Sharon's face turned red. "Don't be silly."

The others laughed.

It was nice to be able to tease her aunt for a change.

Five minutes later, the doorbell rang.

Sharon jumped to her feet. "Will everyone excuse me from the table, please? I bet Bill's here now."

"Of course." Mike grinned and winked at Melody. "I think you've proved your case."

Everyone laughed.

Moments later, Bill and Melody were on their way to McAlester.

Driving, Bill tapped a hand on the steering wheel. "We're taking a scenic route when we get to McAlester. I thought you might enjoy the ride after all the tragedies you experienced. See a new home addition."

"Sounds great."

When they reached the outskirts of McAlester, Melody took in the surroundings: large new homes, well-attended lawns, green shrubbery featuring a variety of colorful flowers.

Melody looked at Bill. "A lot of beautiful homes have been built in this addition."

"They're regular mansions."

By the time they reached McAlester, large and fluffy white clouds laced the clear, blue sky.

After passing the houses, they came to a small café which Melody never saw before. "Looks like McAlester got a new restaurant."

Bill glanced over at the place and frowned. "Yeah, it's only been open a month or so." He jerked his head farther.

"Is something the matter?"

"Nah, nothing." He started driving faster.

She peeked back at the café. In the parking lot set Jordan's car and Kim's vehicle. "Oh, Jordan and Kim are there."

"Probably not. I wouldn't worry about it."

"No, I'm sure it's them. I talked to Kim last night. She said she was meeting Jordan today."

Bill raised his brows. "She did?"

"Yes. Do you know anything about it?"

Bill vigorously shook his head. "I'm, I'm sure it's

business."

"I'm not."

He coughed. "Oh?"

Melody filled him in on what transpired the previous night between Kim and her. She sighed. "I think they may be dating. Have you heard anything about it?"

"No, nothing."

Silence hung in the air for a moment.

She needed to say something. "Listen, Bill, can I level with you? Get something off my chest. It'll be just between us."

Bill nodded. "Of course. I consider you like a daughter Melody, since your father died."

Melody smiled and glanced his way. "I know, and I appreciate our friendship, more than you'll ever know."

Bill reached over and squeezed Melody's hand. "So, what's up?"

He released her hand.

"Ever since I came back to McAlester several months ago, Kim has seemed different."

Turning, Bill raised his eyebrows. "You're not best friends anymore?"

"I thought we were. After last night's phone conversation, I'm not so sure."

Bill sighed. "You've been in Virginia for several years. Sometimes it takes a while to get reacquainted, and the phone call may be nothing. Like I said, it's probably business."

"I doubt it. During the last three years, Kim and I always kept in touch with emails and phone calls. We shared everything until now. And now she's with Jordan…" Melody swallowed hard to keep from crying. "I'm afraid I still have feelings for the guy. The other night I thought perhaps Jordan and I could get back together, highly unlikely now. I wonder if he's okay. His actions sometimes puzzle me. I hope he finds a nice woman for himself, if he hasn't already."

"He did."

The answer was quick, and Melody's heart sank, as her fingers trembled at the information.

She glanced his way. "You mean Kim. Right?"

"No." Bill raised his eyebrows. "Don't you remember the woman who didn't want him, but he wanted her?"

"No, I never knew about it. I wonder what was wrong with the lady. Jordan's one of the finest men I've ever met."

Bill laughed. "Dear, don't you realize the woman I'm talking about was *you*?"

"Oh," she stammered, as she felt her face flush.

She remembered Jordan's kiss from only five nights ago. Now it seemed like an eternity. Especially since she knew he'd never kiss her again.

Chapter 20

After Jordan saw Kim, he got a call to see Captain Scott in his office.

There, he settled on a seat in front of the captain's desk.

Captain Scott folded his large hands and leaned forward in his chair. "I still can't quite believe we came so close to Sonny and Allen last night and never found them."

"Me either. Quite disappointing." Jordan sighed, leaned back and rubbed his neck.

Captain Scott squirmed in his chair. "I think we'll catch them soon though. Officials in Red Oak increased the members of the search party, and we've beefed up things all over Oklahoma now, since we know they haven't left the state."

"Yeah, I think we'll get them sooner or later too. Preferable sooner than later." Jordan picked up a green, coffee mug from the small table by his chair, took a couple gulps and set it down.

Warden Brewer frowned. "How's your injury?"

Jordan rubbed the arm and looked at the captain. "Almost as good as new. Dr. Johnson said my recovery is a miracle."

"Amen." The captain grinned and took a sip of coffee from his nearby cup. "Glad to hear it. Now, what did you find out from your meeting with Kim?

Anything?"

Jordan leaned forward and shook his head. "Yes. You're going to be glad to hear this."

"Oh?" The captain raised his eyebrows.

Jordan nodded. "She's turning out to be an excellent informant. I think the potential drug bust we've been trying to plan for months now may actually take place."

Captain Scott's brown eyes widened. "Seriously?"

Jordan clicked his tongue. "Yup." He reached into his pocket and pulled out a slip of paper. "Here's the names of some people who have been buying from a couple guys who Kim found out have been doing the dealings via some prison connections."

The captain jerked his head. "Like Sonny and Allen?"

"Kim says maybe. The informants working with her don't know for sure, although they suspect it's a possibility."

The captain took the slip and looked over the names. He glanced up at Jordan and grinned. "This is great news."

"Yeah, look at the address on the bottom of the paper."

Looking at the paper, the warden rubbed his chin. "I know where the place is. What about it?"

"Seems like one of Kim's AA friends said he heard his old dealer just got out of prison and is back to dealing again at an old run-down house at that address. Kim wants to go there undercover and make a buy, with police backup, of course, for protection and so we can arrest some bad guys."

Captain Scott slapped his hands on the table and laughed. "Sure, we can. Do you know the dealer's name?"

Jordan shook his head. "He goes by the nickname of Catfish. Apparently, he loves to eat the stuff. The AA friend, who used to buy from him, doesn't know his real name, said he never uses it."

"In any case, we've got some bad guys out there. We may be able to make some arrests."

Jordan gave a firm nod. "I agree."

"Who knows? If Sonny and Allen aren't caught by then, maybe we'll find them when Kim makes her buy."

Jordan chuckled. "I've seen stranger things happen in this business." He leaned back in his chair and crossed his hands behind his head.

Captain Scott rose from his desk and slapped a hand on Jordan's shoulder. "Come on. Hope you're not too tired. I want to gather some officers for the drug bust now."

Coming to full alert, Jordan hopped off the chair and felt a new surge of energy bolt through his body. "Coming."

An hour later, in the conference room, about a dozen police officers sat around a large, conference table.

Jordan and Captain Scott stood in front.

The captain folded his arms. "Lieutenant Lakewater just got some great information from our informant Kim. We're organizing a drug bust for tomorrow evening. I know it's quick, but Kim just got information on a place where a big shipment of cocaine may have arrived at this address."

Captain Scott wrote the address on a whiteboard. "A lot of people may be planning to go there tomorrow evening to buy some of the stuff. If such is the case, we will probably be able to make some arrests. People either using or selling drugs." The captain nodded to Jordan. "Tell them the rest."

Jordan cleared his throat and, in minutes, pointed out the residence on a large McAlester map and gave the men their assignments. "Just a quick reminder, everyone. We're going to either arrest the guys we catch or take them to juvenile hall, depending on their age. A few minors may be involved."

Afterwards, the captain conducted a question and answer period and then excused the officers.

The next day, outside, the local police went to their assigned cars to begin the drug bust they wanted to make for so long.

Late, afternoon sunshine drifted through nearby trees. As Jordan climbed into the undercover vehicle, an old Chevy, he wondered if the beauty of the moment was a sign everything was going to be okay. He hoped police would be able to make all the arrests as planned, including Sonny and Allen. If the bust was successful, it'd be a tremendous achievement in alleviating the drug activity in McAlester. It may even solve a murder case or two which occurred, since the Cobras slowly and slyly wormed into the community.

Moments later, Captain Scott eased the Chevy to the side of the road, near an old home. He looked at Jordan. "This must be the place."

Jordan nodded.

Kim rolled by ahead of them in another undercover car, an old beat up Ford. She parked and cracked down her window.

A guy with oily, dark hair popped out of the house and raced to her vehicle. Jordan watched Kim speak to the man. Seconds later, the guy slipped a small, brown package in her hand. She took it and handed him some money.

"We've got this one! Let's go!" the captain whispered.

In minutes, the guy was arrested and hauled off by a couple other policemen.

Jordan and the captain dashed up the steps of the dilapidated house. Jordan knocked on the door.

No answer.

"Police!" Captain Scott yelled. "Let us in."

Again, no one answered.

The officers flung themselves against the old, wooden door and knocked it down. Other policemen followed them.

A reddish-haired man, wearing torn, blue jeans with large holes, popped in the hallway. "Hey, man, what's going on? You can't just barge in here."

Captain Scott slammed his hands on his hips. "We certainly can. We're the police."

"Why didn't you answer the door when we knocked?" Jordan inquired. "What're you hiding from?"

"Nothing, man, nothing."

Jordan grinned and turned to the guy, with blonde hair, coming out of the bathroom. "How about you? Are you hiding anything, like drugs?"

The guy ran a hand through his hair. "No way. I never take the stuff."

"Do you deal drugs?" Captain Scott raised his eyebrows.

The red-headed guy said, "We're clean."

Jordan showed the two men a search warrant. "We'll see."

After some arguing, Jordan and the captain got the

guys to identify themselves: Bruce Peterson and Lucas Furemore.

"Furemore!" Jordan exclaimed. "You must be related to Sonny." He looked at Lucas.

"How'd you know?"

Jordan shrugged and grinned. "Lucky guess."

"A good one." Captain Scott gave Jordan's back a hearty slap.

Bruce glared at Lucas. "You dummy! I told ya' you talk too much."

"Tell us where Sonny's at," the captain demanded.

Lucas' face turned white, and he shook his head. "Hey, man, I don't know."

Captain Scott gave a sarcastic chuckle. "Yeah, you do. We heard Sonny and Leo were hanging out here. Now where are they?"

Bruce raised his voice. "We don't know. Honest."

Lucas' blue eyes widened. "We were hoping they'd come here."

Bruce doubled his fists. "Lucas!"

Lucas nervously shook his head. "I-I-I mean I don't know."

"Too late." Jordan looked at the captain. "Looks like we'll need to hang out here." He turned to the other officers standing behind him. "Start searching."

Bruce spread out his arms. "Be my guest. You ain't gonna find anything."

"Then you've got nothing to worry about." Jordan nodded at them.

The officers scrambled to every room and found guys hiding everywhere: under beds, in closets and upstairs. All of them claimed no drugs were in the house.

Police kept searching. They overturned sofa

cushions and bed mattresses. They scanned dresser drawers and detailed closets. During the commotion, Jordan cleared out every item in one closet for inspection, including a jump rope, a heavy one. He wondered what the rope was used for. And why was it so heavy? He handed the rope to Captain Scott.

"Here captain, take this. Tell me what you think."

Grabbing the cord, Captain Scott shook his head. "Whew! It's heavy." He looked at Bruce and Lucas. "What do you guys use this for?"

"Exercise." Bruce grinned. "We keep in shape."

Lucas frowned and looked at Bruce.

"Who does it belong to?" Jordan wanted to know.

Bruce rubbed his hands on his jeans. "Lucas."

Lucas jerked his head Bruce's way. "You bought it."

Captain Scott sighed and placed his hands on his hips. "Which is it?"

Silence.

"Where'd you buy it?" Jordan asked.

Bruce shrugged and raked a hand through his hair. "Man, it's been so long ago. I don't remember."

The captain put his hands on his hips. "Your best bet is to level with us. What's in the rope?"

Lucas looked at Bruce and then Captain Scott and Jordan.

Bruce shrugged. "What'd ya'll mean? It's just a rope."

"So, why is it so heavy?" Jordan frowned.

"Who knows? I don't make the things." Bruce gave a smug smile.

Captain Scott rolled the rope over in his hands. "Did you put anything in the rope?"

Bruce snickered. "What on earth could anyone put

in a rope?"

Jordan looked at Bruce. "Don't play dumb with us." He turned toward Captain Scott. "What do you think is in the rope, captain? Perhaps liquid cocaine?"

Bruce and Luca's faces turned white at the same time.

Bruce gave a nervous laugh. "The dumbest thing I ever heard. Ain't no cocaine in the rope. I'm tellin' ya."

Jordan grabbed a jack knife from his pocket. "Well, let's just find out." He punched a hole in the rope.

Several drops of liquid popped to the surface.

The captain laughed and looked at Bruce and Lucas. "Okay, guys, better start leveling with us. We know it's liquid cocaine."

"No, ya' don't. Ya'll can't be sure of somethin' like that," Bruce snarled.

Lucas snickered and crossed his arms. "Yeah."

Jordan sighed. "We can't be one hundred percent certain. So, let's just find out. Shall we?"

The captain nodded. "Go for it."

Bruce snorted. "Whatever. You ain't gonna find nothin'."

The captain cleared his throat. "Look, guys, this is your last chance to talk. You have anything you want to say?"

Bruce crossed his arms. "No, man, I'm clean. How 'bout you, Lucas? Do you have somethin' to say?"

Lucas looked at Bruce. "N-N-No. Not one thing. I'm innocent."

"We'll see." Jordan pulled out a cocaine, test strip and squeezed a dab of the substance from the rope. The strip turned colors. "It's positive."

Bruce madly shook his head. "We didn't put nothin'

in the rope. I don't know how it got there."

"Tell the judge that," Jordan said.

He handcuffed Bruce while Captain Scott snapped another set of metal links on Lucas.

Outside, Jordan held his hand on Bruce's head to help get him in the car.

"Be careful," Jordan said.

Bruce gave Jordan an icy glare. "If ya' think you're getting away with this, you're crazy!"

Lucas glared at Jordan and the captain. "Right on, man. My cuz's gonna catch up with you guys."

Bruce snickered. "Yeah, he'll show you whose boss."

Jordan stared at the two guys. "Don't count on it."

Captain Scott nodded. "You're underestimating the police. We're determined to find them, one way or the other. You can tell us anytime."

Lucas squirmed in his seat. "We don't know where Sonny and Allen are at. They were supposed to have showed up here two hours ago."

"Shut up!" Bruce howled. "You've gotta stop talkin' so much."

Chapter 21

Hours later, Melody watched the late evening news on television. A broadcast journalist reported, "Twenty-four people were arrested in a McAlester drug bust today. Meanwhile, two Oklahoma State Penitentiary prison escapees, from last week's riot, remain at large."

The reporter went on to give information about Sonny and Allen.

Melody snapped off the remote. She didn't want to hear any more for now. She started pacing in the living room. Aunt Sharon and the Hendricks went to bed long ago. Melody knew sleep was out of the question for her. Jordan still wasn't home. Was he helping officers look for Sonny and Allen? Or was he perhaps with Kim? And why did she care so much?

She plopped back down on the soft recliner and took several deep breaths. She needed to relax. She closed her heavy eyelids. Later, she heard the back kitchen door open. She tossed forward in her chair and opened her eyes at the same time. She glanced at her watch. One o'clock in the morning. Apparently, she slept for at least an hour.

Jordan strolled in the living room. He raised his eyebrows. "You're still up."

"Yes. I'm afraid I had trouble getting to sleep." She leaned forward and rubbed her eyes. "I eventually got the job done though. I can't believe it's early morning already."

Jordan gave a moan. "I'm sorry I woke you."

She shook her head and ran fingers through her hair. She hoped she wasn't a mess. "It's okay. No problem. Congratulations on the drug bust."

"Thanks. You heard."

She nodded. "I listened to part of the evening news. I'm sorry to hear you didn't get Sonny and Allen. I'm really happy about the other guys though."

Jordan raked a hand through his black hair. "Yeah, the officers are pretty excited about the arrests, and we've beefed up security a lot in hopes of finding Sonny and Allen."

"Good." Melody felt calmer now. No doubt, from the hour sleep she got. She also figured the serenity came from knowing Jordan was safe again. Now why? She knew there was no hope for the two of them, since he was seeing Kim. He made it clear with their final kiss. Of course, she cared about the guy's safety. Even so, did her concerns for his physical health go beyond something else? Like love? If so, she needed to get rid of those feelings since Kim entered the picture.

She gave her head a shake.

"Something wrong?" Jordan frowned.

She flipped her hands. "I'm fine." She studied him for a moment. "Is it too late for a cup of hot chocolate before you go to bed?"

His dark eyes widened. "What a great idea. I'm pretty keyed up right now, excited over the accomplishments made in the drug bust and, on the other hand, I'm frustrated we didn't get Sonny and Allen. Hot chocolate sounds soothing."

In the kitchen, Melody got some milk and a can of

whipped cream from the refrigerator and then retrieved a container of powered chocolate from the cupboard. Jordan took a seat on the high kitchen chair by the bar. "So, how was your day?"

She poured a chocolate mixture into the cups. "Good. I'm glad I went back to work, gives me time to get my mind off things I'm worried about." She placed the prepared cups in the microwave.

He nodded. "Care to talk about it?"

Sighing, she took a seat by him. "I've felt so unsettled lately, since the riot. My mind seems to be going in a million directions at once."

He placed a hand on her arm. "I'm a good listener."

She wiped some tears dripping slowly down her face.

He put his arm around her. "What is it?"

She shook her head.

Ding. She headed for the microwave.

"Sit down. I'll get it." Jordan was already on his way.

She resumed her seat. He set the two steaming cups of liquid on the yellow counter bar and sat back down by her. "Continue."

She turned his way and attempted to read his thoughts. His face looked attentive, concerned. Did he still care about her a little? Or was his heart completely wrapped around Kim?

She took a deep breath and shook her head. "I'm just so mixed up about everything. I don't know where to start."

He grinned and cupped her chin. "Begin by telling me one thing you're worried about."

Us! She refrained from saying it.

She shook her head, waved her hand, and took a sip of chocolate. "I don't want to burden you."

He chuckled. "You won't be. Please, tell me. What's bothering you?"

"I'm okay. Really. It's late, and I'm overthinking."

He gave her shoulder a quick squeeze, took a gulp of the hot liquid, looked back at her and grinned. "Oh, come on, we're friends."

She took another sip of her drink. "I probably shouldn't say anything, but I was finally able to talk to Kim. We visited for a long time the other night. I'm still worried about her. She sounded so distant."

"I wouldn't worry. You and she have a lot going on since the riot. One of the inmates she was working with died, you know."

"Yes, Warden Brewer told me about it. I told her I was sorry."

"I'm sure your sympathy meant a lot to her."

"I'm not so sure."

He frowned. "Why would you say such a thing?"

"Just the way she sounded."

"Kim's got a lot on her mind. I wouldn't worry if I were you. Kim will come around in time. You're such good friends."

She looked at Jordan. "I don't know if we can be friends anymore."

"Why on earth would you say such a thing?"

Melody shrugged. "She's so different now."

"Don't forget. She needed to make a lot of adjustments because of the riot."

Melody nodded. Jordan seemed so concerned about Kim. Still, why wouldn't he be? He apparently was in love with the woman.

Jordan grinned and looked at her. "I know what we need to do."

"What?"

"Let's go to the Fall Festival this weekend. I think you'd love it."

Melody's fingers trembled as she wrapped them around her cup. "Aren't you going with Kim?"

"No, she doesn't want to get out in public right now. Come on. What do you say?"

Melody sighed and recalled the past McAlester festivals she'd been to before she moved to Virginia. "I do like those types of things."

Why did he ask her when he dated Kim? He'd just said they were friends, she reminded herself. Maybe that was it. She knew he was grateful for her help in the riot. And, from the way things looked, he would always claim she saved his life.

Jordan laughed. "So you'll go?"

"Yes. I'll tell Kim first though. See if it's okay with her."

Jordan frowned and shrugged. "Whatever." He leaned toward her and held her shoulders.

"Good night," he whispered.

He leaned forward. Was he going to kiss her? Surely not. Her imagination kept running away from her. She needed to get in bed before she went totally insane with her crazy thoughts. She slipped away from his personal space and nodded. "Good night."

She didn't know if it was her imagination or not, but she thought he frowned for a brief second. She rose from her chair.

He stood up. "Good night."

She turned, strolled upstairs and went to bed.

The next day, during noon break, Melody arranged to call Kim. She didn't want any misunderstandings. Melody decided to be civil to both Jordan and her. After all, the two were never mean to her. Besides, people fell in love all the time, and she turned down Jordan's proposal long ago. She never expected the guy to stay single because of her, and Kim was a great woman. She sighed. Of course, she never imagined he'd fall for her best friend. She needed to squelch her jealous feeling over the issue. No way did she want to be miserable the rest of her life. On the other hand, how could she be happy again?

Without Jordan?

She punched Kim's contact.

"Hello."

"Hi Kim. I'm sorry to call, because I know the warden wants you to keep your line as free as possible, but may I talk to you for just a minute."

"Yes. What is it?"

"Jordan asked me to go the Fall Festival this weekend, and I was wondering if you cared if I went?"

"No, of course not. It's a great idea."

"He said he'd asked you first."

"He's being so kind to me. He knows how terrible I felt after the riot. He wanted to stay here and keep me company too. I told him to go and have a good time."

"Kim—"

"Yes?"

"Don't you think Jordan's acting a little strange?"

"What? I'm not sure I understand."

"Why exactly would Jordan ask me to go? Aren't your feelings hurt?"

"No, of course not. Why do you even ask?"

"Because I know you've been seeing him."

Kim chuckled. "I understand men, and I would think you would too."

So, Kim understood men.

The words stabbed Melody's heart. Was the statement made on purpose, as a cruel reminder Melody didn't understand guys years ago, when she confided in Kim that she simply couldn't marry Jordan, for fear of living in danger, not knowing from one day to the next if her loved one would survive a work shift? And, if Kim made the statement on purpose, why did she?

"Melody, I've got to go. I have an incoming call. We'll catch up later."

"Okay."

When Melody hung up the phone, a heaviness fell over her. She wondered if anything would ever be the same again.

****

The next evening, in bed, Jordan tossed and turned. He'd wanted to kiss Melody again. On the lips. Even though he'd told her that he wouldn't. If women could change their minds, why couldn't he? His mind flashed back to the awkward situation the other night. Why did she back up from the start of his embrace, after their chocolate cup conversation? For some crazy reason, he hoped she'd simply fall in his arms and allow another kiss from him, an even more intimate one. She'd pulled away like a frightened child. Why? What did he do wrong?

Perhaps she didn't have any residue feelings from their relationship.

He turned in bed and slammed a fist on his pillow. He decided to find out exactly how she felt about him.

Someway, somehow. He needed to, in order to have any peace of mind. And then, even if by some miracle her feelings were mutual, he'd have to tell her the details surrounding her father's death. He'd have to find out if she could still love him after his involvement in her father's death. Such a huge risk. If she didn't love him, he'd have to face facts. She was a free woman. He couldn't force her into marrying him, nor would he ever do such a thing. To him, matrimony was a fully embraced commitment between both parties, not one.

Groaning, he turned over and eventually went to sleep.

The next day, brilliant sunlight flowed across the crowd, gathered outdoors for a barbecue at the festival, held in Chadick Park. Fluffy clouds drifted across the clear, blue sky with gentle winds prevailing.

Laughter filled the air as people visited. Children played on swings, slides and monkey bars. Teens engaged in tennis and other games while adults gathered in groups to visit.

Jordan sat by Melody on a bench, shaded by some trees. White and pink flowers bloomed nearby. A gentle breeze whirled across his face as he took her hand. Was it his imagination or were her hands trembling?

He raised his eyebrows. "Enjoying yourself?"

"Yes, it's a beautiful day." Slowly, she pulled her hand away from his.

He frowned. "Something wrong?"

She shook her head and gave a nervous giggle. "No, nothing."

He didn't believe her.

****

Sonny and Allen rode in a black sedan. Driving,

Sonny pulled the vehicle and parked in a group of trees across the street, about a hundred yards from the park.

Allen pointed toward the car clock.

"It's nearly noon and no action!" he shouted to Sonny. "What happened to our bomb? Why didn't it go off?"

Sonny grabbed the front of Allen's black tee-shirt. "Look, get wise with me, and you're dead meat!"

"I'm your bro. You wouldn't take one of your own down."

Still holding Allen's tee-shirt in a knot, Sonny hissed, "Don't be so sure. You obviously messed things up!"

"Me!" Allen shouted back in Sonny's face. He yanked his shirt free from Sonny's large hands. "You're the one who designed the thing."

"Wise guy, you were the one who helped. You obviously did somethin' wrong!"

"Hey, Boss Man, calm down!" Allen added some swear words.

Sonny grabbed Allen's wrist and twisted it. "How do you expect me to chill out when you goofed?"

"Ouch! Let me go, man. It hurts."

"Oh, poooor baby." Sonny yanked and twisted Allen's wrist harder. "Take that!"

Pulling away from Sonny, Allen grabbed his wrist and rubbed it. "I'm not going to take all the blame. Perhaps both of us did somethin' wrong."

"I doubt it. I've done this before."

Allen snapped his fingers and turned to Sonny. "Did ya' ever do it during Daylight Savings time?"

Sonny gave a huge wheeze, slammed his fists on the steering wheel and glared at Allen. "We forgot to set the bomb for an hour later. Why'd you forget such a thing?"

"Why'd you forget?" Allen snapped back.

Slowly, Sonny exhaled, leaned back on the seat, closed his eyes and whispered, "Wait a minute, dummy. What're we arguin' fer?" He opened his eyes and grinned.

Allen groaned. "I don't see what there is to smile about."

"Think! It'll still go off, just later is all."

Allen started laughing.

"Shhhhhhh, dude, keep it down. We don't want anyone to hear us."

"Right, Boss Man. Right. Only twenty-five minutes before the fireworks."

Sonny snickered as he did the gang hand symbol with Allen. "That'll give us just enough time to get outta here so we don't get hurt. Then we can come back later to see the damage we caused. If Melody and Jordan are still alive, we'll have to take 'em down."

Allen snickered. "I love the way ya' think, Boss Man."

Chapter 22

Jordan gently placed his arm across Melody's back. She sunk into the warmth of his body, remembering how many times he placed his arm around her waist before. She enjoyed his body heat so much that, for a moment, she feared they were doing something wrong. Then she remembered, only too well, Jordan and Kim were a twosome now. She wasn't about to try to do anything to break their relationship. She'd never do such a thing to her friends. Besides, Jordan was simply being friendly with her. So she allowed him to lead her to the food tents and enjoyed the moment.

He leaned over and kissed the top of her head. "I've been looking forward to today."

Her body stiffened. Didn't she realize his kisses sent her heart spinning, and he shouldn't do actions which could hurt Kim?

Two lines formed to go inside the tent. Melody and Jordan stood in the back.

He grinned at her and winked. "I've arranged for a small table for the two of us to sit. It'll be a little more private."

If she didn't know him so well, she would have thought he was flirting. He couldn't be, not with Kim in the picture.

Inside the tent, Jordan took a red, plastic plate and silverware and handed it to Melody.

"Thanks." She took the dinner utensils.

Pots of casseroles, beans, pot roast and vegetable trays set with a variety of salads and desserts. Aunt Sharon made an impressive array with her contributions of potato salad, a tray of cold cuts and cheese and a rich-looking chocolate cake.

They dished up their food and took their place at a small table in a corner. A cool breeze blew through a side screened opening in the tent.

Melody smiled as she sat down and set her plate on the table. "It's nice here. Perfect."

He grinned and took a seat opposite her.

Melody took a bit of salad greens. "This is delicious."

"So is my potato salad." He looked at her. "Your aunt must have made it."

"She did."

"Give her my compliments."

"I will."

Melody frowned, wishing she could be more than friends with Jordan.

He gazed at her. "I wish you'd tell me what's bothering you."

Suddenly, her face felt steaming hot. Melody realized Jordan could still read her mind. She took a deep breath. Did she dare ask if Kim and he were planning a future together? Slowly, she inhaled, set down her fork and placed her hands together in a twisted knot on her lap.

"Listen, Jordan, you don't have to be so polite and nice to me any longer. The good times we experienced together are over. I know that and so do you."

Suddenly, Melody felt the ground shake.

Boom!

"Oh, my God!" she whispered in disbelief.

In front of them, from the open end of the tent, a large red and orange ball of fire whirled through the air. Wooden debris and glass flew in every direction. Everyone dove to the floor from the impact.

Seconds later, Jordan stood before her and took her hand. "Let me help you up."

"How'd you get back on your feet so quickly?"

"Comes from training." He grinned.

Taking his hand, Melody stood. Hunks of grass and dirt stuck to her long, red hair.

Jordan looked at her. "Are you okay?"

"Yes. How about you?"

"Yeah, I'm good."

Confusion hung in the atmosphere as everyone asked everyone what happened. Some people bled and yelled in pain.

Jordan grabbed his cell from his pocket, snapped the device open and pushed a button. "Captain, a bomb just exploded at the festival. I'm with Melody. We need EMT's, rescue and security."

Melody wrung her hands together. When Jordan got off the cell, she asked, "Did the Cobras strike again?"

He nodded. "Looks like it. Thankfully, the undercover agents are with us since we beefed up security."

She scanned the crowd. Then she stopped dead in her tracks. A foot ahead of her were Sonny and Allen. They both rushed toward Jordan and herself with wicked grins on their faces.

She couldn't believe what was happening. First, the bomb and now Sonny and Allen were actually here, standing only a few feet from Jordan and her. Approaching both of them!

With precision, Sonny and Allen each flashed a knife in front of them. A man grabbed her from behind. Her heart raced, making her feel like the vital organ moved up her throat.

"Don't worry, Melody," the man behind her whispered. "It's one of the undercover agents."

He gave his name. She wasn't sure if he was telling her the truth or not. She didn't recognize the name. Of course, she wouldn't know everyone who was working undercover today.

Bang! A gunshot echoed behind her. The man, who'd identified himself as being undercover, fell against her, pushing Melody to the ground. Someone in the crowd apparently shot him. Struggling, she crawled several feet to get out from under the man, regained her balance and get back on her feet. Turning, she saw a guy with a Cobra tattoo on his arm. He held a gun and headed her direction. *Is he going to shoot me? Or kidnap me?* He jumped in front of her. She grabbed a small can of tear gas from her purse, strapped over her shoulder. She sprayed the Cobra in the eyes. He choked and stumbled backward, shoving people every which way. He fell to the ground. Screams echoed through the crowd.

Allen now stood in front of her. Immediately, she sprayed his eyes too. He gave her the same reaction as the other Cobra. The knife fell from his hand. She turned to Sonny to give him tear gas too. Sonny was ready to stab Jordan in the chest. When Melody pushed the button on her tear gas can, no spray emerged. The can was empty.

She wondered where the other undercover security

men were. Why hadn't anyone else appeared to help them? A number of men in the crowd were leading other people away from everyone. Perhaps the undercover agents spotted some other Cobras and were going to arrest them. Or, on the other hand, did the Cobras find out who the undercover agents were? Maybe the gang members were kidnapping law enforcement. Melody knew gangs could obtain tremendous power with the right weapons, and she was seeing a lot of men holding sharp shanks which could kill in seconds.

She spotted the gun the man dropped when she'd sprayed him with tear gas. Before she could get to the weapon, however, another guy grabbed it.

Smack! She turned to see blood drip from Sonny's bottom lip. Jordan's fists curled tight. *Smack!* Jordan hit Sonny again. Sonny rammed into Jordan. He held his knife to Jordan's throat. Melody saw Jordan grab Sonny's hand that held the knife. The two began battling ferociously.

****

Pain enveloped Jordan's body with a stinging rage. His injured arm felt heavier than the rest of his body. He saw Sonny come at him with the knife. *Whish!* Jordan felt the nearness of Sonny's arm swing. He'd ducked in time. He swung at Sonny with his fist.

From the corner of his eye, Jordan saw a guy hold up a bowl of potato salad and—*swish!*—crash it on a man's head. Potato salad and pieces of glass poured from the bowl and splattered among the crowd. The man fell to the ground, and an undercover agent handcuffed him. Even with similar activity throughout the mass of people, Jordan knew he couldn't afford to lose focus. He lifted his leg to kick Sonny in the groin. This time Sonny got him in the stomach first. A nearby guy threw a bowl of hot beans toward Sonny, making the shank fall from his hand.

Quickly Jordan accessed the situation. If he hurried, he could hit Sonny before he retrieved his knife. If the shank was within his reach, he could grab the weapon and attack Sonny, but it was not. Doubling a fist, Jordan hit Sonny in the stomach, knocking the wind out of him. Sonny fell to the ground.

"You're going to be sorry you did that!" Sonny roared to Jordan.

Jordan hoped an undercover agent would be able to give him a hand in the fight. He knew though the other officers were too busy fighting and capturing the bad guys in the crowd, Cobras who'd burst on the scene.

Ambulances and police sirens kept screeching as more and more men arrived on the scene, law men to help capture all of the Cobras and medical personnel to take the wounded to the hospital. Sonny rose to his feet and raced to the knife. Jordan made a mad dash to get behind Sonny. Quickly, Sonny swooped the knife in his hand. Jordan jumped and landed on Sonny's back, with extreme force, which surprised even Jordan.

Sonny hollered, "You're not gonna get away with this!"

Jordan struggled to get the knife out of Sonny's hand. The two bodies twisted around each other as they fought. Jordan saw the foot of a woman, wearing a sharp heel, bash down on Sonny's hand. It was Melody.

Chapter 23

Melody grabbed the knife and kept her foot on Sonny. A gunshot ran through the air, throwing her to the ground. She jumped back on her feet.

"Owwwwww!" Sonny screamed, as he stumbled to an upright position. Blood poured from his leg.

Melody grabbed him, in his weakened state, and held the shank to his throat. "Don't move."

Jordan rushed to her.

Still holding the weapon, she smiled at Jordan. "I thought you could use some help."

Jordan grinned. "Thanks." He retrieved a pair of handcuffs inside his coat pocket and handcuffed Sonny.

Sonny glared at Melody. "I need medical help."

Melody smiled. "I agree. You're getting it at the prison."

Sonny let out a string of swear words.

Other officers took him and headed back to the prison.

Melody scanned the crowd. "Where's Allen?"

An undercover agent stood nearby. He looked at her. "I handcuffed him, thanks to you." He turned to Jordan. "Fortunately, the tear gas Melody sprayed on Allen made it possible for me to make the capture."

Jordan's eyebrows rose and he turned to Melody. "Great work." He slid his arm around her waist. "You've turned into quite a prison worker. Your father would be proud."

The compliment pleased her more than she could say. She gave him a wide smile. "Thanks."

Melody looked at the agent. "Is Allen on his way back to prison, like Sonny?"

The official grinned. "Sure is. We also caught and arrested ten other Cobras in this madness."

Melody gave a big sigh. "Good news. Things in McAlester may be able to return back to normal now."

"Looks like it." Jordan winked at her.

Her heart bounced. Immediately, she shook her head and reminded herself Jordan loved Kim now. For good.

During the next week, Melody, her aunt and the Hendricks left the witness protection program and resettled in the Hendrick home. Both Mr. and Mrs. Hendrick continued to extend their hospitality to Melody and her aunt.

The past several evenings, Melody and Aunt Sharon searched newspapers and called reality companies to check on the homes available for sale in McAlester. They selected three possibilities.

During this time, Melody didn't see Jordan since the bomb explosion. No doubt they'd remain apart. She never told anyone, but she ached beyond measure without him. Several times she even picked up her cell to call him, see how he was doing. She refrained each time. She couldn't do such a thing to Kim.

However, she made it a point to keep her friendship with Kim. They talked daily. Their conversations didn't include Jordan. Melody wanted to wish Kim well with Jordan in her life now. Every time Melody attempted to express warm wishes, however, she choked on the words and tears stung her eyes. Perhaps, Melody thought, things were better this way.

Then, Friday evening, everyone was visiting in the living room when the doorbell rang.

"I'll get it." Melody rose from her chair.

She strolled across the living room, kitchen and back entrance. There, she opened the door. Jordan stood on the back porch. He held a bouquet of red roses and babies' breath.

Melody gasped. "Jordan! It's nice to see you again."

"Thanks. I'm on my way to work, and I wanted to drop these off." He handed her the flowers.

She took the fresh bouquet. "Thank you."

This time she wasn't going to make the same assumption she'd made when Jordan brought flowers for her aunt.

"Come on in, and I'll give these to Aunt Sharon. She'll be thrilled."

He chuckled. "The flowers are for you, and there's a note with them. I've gotta get to work. The captain's waiting for me. I'll call tonight to get your answer to the note."

"Thank you so much. I love roses."

"I remember."

He dashed down the porch steps, got in his car and sped off.

In the kitchen, Melody set the flowers on the table and removed the note from the bouquet. She flipped the small card open.

"After everything we've been through, I'd love to take you out for a nice dinner tonight in a new restaurant. Kim and I ate there a few times and loved it. How about it? I've got to be on call, but we can still have a good time. With all my love, Jordan."

Apparently he wanted to say he was serious about Kim. Her first thought was not to go for fear the evening would be too difficult emotionally. Still, if he wanted to tell her about Kim, she needed to hear what he had to say. To make things easier for both of them. She would go. And tell him good-by.

Sharon entered the kitchen.

Melody jumped at the intrusion. "I'm sorry, auntie. You scared me."

"Oh my, I didn't mean to. Who was at the door?"

"Jordan."

Sharon's eyes twinkled. "How is he?"

"Fine."

Sharon looked at the roses. "What lovely flowers."

Melody cleared her throat. "I'm afraid they're for me."

"I didn't think they were for me this time." Sharon laughed. "They're beautiful. I see there's a card by them." She looked at Melody and gave her one of those I-think-Cupid-is-at-work looks.

Melody flipped her hands. "Now, don't go making anything out of it."

Picking up the flowers from the table, Melody took them to the sink, removed the paper wrapping and placed the blossoms in a white vase. She set the arrangement on the table.

Melody cleared her throat. "If you can get along without me this evening, I'm going to have dinner with Jordan."

Folding her hands, Sharon smiled. "I'll be fine. Don't forget the Hendricks are here if I need anything. Why, you and Jordan can take all the time in the world to have a great time."

Shaking her head, Melody rubbed her hands on her hips. "It's nothing like you think. This is a good-bye dinner. Jordan's seeing Kim now."

Frowning, Sharon sat down at the table. "Seriously?"

Sighing, Melody took a seat also. "I'm afraid so."

Sharon sighed. "I'm so sorry——"

"Don't be," Melody interrupted. "Think about it. Kim's a great woman."

"I didn't mean——"

"I want to be sensible about this whole situation," Melody cut in again. "I admit I spent a night or two crying about it."

"Why do you think they're seeing each other?"

"Two reasons."

"Yes?" Sharon peered over her glasses.

"Number one, Bill and I saw them at the diner on the outskirts of town. Number two, when I asked Jordan about it, he said he'd been seeing Kim. Look at the card he sent."

Melody shoved the note her aunt's way.

Sharon picked it up and read it. When she finished, she looked up at her niece. "This doesn't mean anything."

Melody spread her arms apart. "Of course it does. Why else would they be eating at a restaurant?"

"I don't know. I suggest you look at how he sighed the card."

Melody snatched the card from her aunt and reread the note. "With all my love. So?"

"So, I think the man's in love with you!"

Melody shook her head. "Don't be ridiculous."

Sharon took her niece's hand. "Hon, I think you're

the one being silly. You're jumping to conclusions." Her aunt released her hand and leaned back in her chair. "I love you like a daughter."

"And I love you like a mother."

Sharon frowned. "Jordan seems really interested in you."

Melody gave a giggle. "I think you're imagining things the way you want to. You always loved Jordan, but Kim and him have a right to feel about each other the way they apparently do. I don't expect either of them to keep their distance just because I'm back in McAlester and still love the guy."

Aunt Sharon's eyebrows rose. "So you admit it?"

A couple tears rolled down Melody's cheeks. She nodded. "During all this madness with the riot and everything, I came to that conclusion. I'll brush the feelings aside. I've got to." She pulled a tissue from her pocket and wiped her tears.

Aunt Sharon leaned forward and glanced at the bouquet. "A man just doesn't buy flowers to tell a girl good-bye."

"I couldn't figure it out at first either. Think about it. Jordan gives me credit for saving his life and—"

"You did." Her aunt interrupted this time.

Melody sighed. "I'm just glad the two of us could help each other in the circumstances."

She didn't say anything further to her aunt. She replayed their conversation in her head over and over. Could it be possible? Could she actually have another chance with Jordan?

Hours later, Melody and Jordan sat at a small table in Cozy Diner. They ordered halibut steak. Moments later, the waiter brought two bowls of salad greens with cherry tomatoes, black Greek olives and feta cheese.

Jordan grinned. "I love the red dress you're wearing and your earrings."

She couldn't even blush. She wondered why Jordan said such a thing when he was seeing Kim? On second thought, she realized he probably meant nothing by it. Maybe she was like her aunt, imagining things that she wanted to be. She returned to her salad and turned the conversation to small chit chat as they ate.

She waited for him to bring up the subject of Kim. He didn't. He talked about their great times together when they dated. At the memories, he even got her laughing at some of the silly stuff they did.

"Sounds like you're having a good time," the waiter said, carrying two plates with halibut steaks. He set the dinner plates in front of them.

Jordan laughed. "We were talking about one time when we went to a Halloween party in high school. We didn't recognize each other until everyone identified themselves before we went home."

The waiter laughed. "May I ask who each of you were?"

"I went as Frankenstein and she looked like Mrs. Frankenstein."

Melody laughed, even though the word "Mrs." stung her heart. She imagined the happy life she could have experienced as Mrs. Lakewater. Shaking her head, she squelched the memory. She couldn't afford to think that way.

When the server returned to his duties, Melody took a bite of her halibut. "Um, this tastes great too. It's so tender."

"Like you." He winked.

She studied his face. What was he getting at? Was he trying to make her feel good before he told her about Kim?

For dessert, they ordered two chocolate mousse.

Several moments later, the waiter set two parfait glasses, filled with the dessert, topped with whipped cream and several chocolate curls, on the table.

"Enjoy." The server gave a brief nod and grin, then dashed to another table.

Melody took a spoonful of the rich sweet. "Umm, this is wonderful."

Jordan grinned. "Just like you."

Now why did he say that? Some of his comments seemed so out of place, considering his relationship with Kim.

She looked around the room and then at him. "This is really a nice place." She wanted to change the subject.

"I wanted somewhere romantic. I wanted this evening to be special."

What on earth was the man doing? Melody wondered if he told Kim the same lines. And, if so, why was he doing this to her? She frowned.

He took her hand. "Melody, what am I doing wrong?"

"Is it obvious?" She fought back tears.

"Uh hum. Afraid so. You look very upset with me. What is it?"

His cell rang. "I'm sorry. I've got to answer the phone. You know I'm on call."

She nodded. "Yes, I understand."

When he finished the call, he looked at her. "I'm afraid I can't tell you about what's going on until everything's done. Duty calls. I need to take you home early."

She smiled. "I understand. Really. No problem."

****

Jordan realized Melody changed. From her actions, he could tell she wasn't afraid, like she used to be when he went on police business. She'd make a wonderful policeman's wife now. He wondered if she knew that.

After he took her home, they got out of the car. Jordan wrapped his arm around her shoulders. "Are you cold?"

She turned to him with a puzzled look. "No."

"I thought with the fall weather, you may be chilly without a sweater. We're supposed to get a thunderstorm tonight." He gave her shoulders a squeeze.

When they got to the porch, he leaned forward. "I really enjoyed tonight." Moonbeams shone on her face. He leaned so close to her their faces nearly touched. He cupped his hands around her chin and pulled her even closer. His heart beat against his chest as he swept his arms across her back.

Chapter 24

Melody felt her heart race. Was he going to kiss her?

Beams of moonlight fell across his face. Melody knew she could pull back. She even tried to, but her body wasn't obeying her commands. Instead of moving away from him, she slid toward his chest. His spicy scent, smelling fresh and clean, stirred all kinds of sensations in her. Her breath shortened. Perhaps he was seeing Kim on business after all. On the other hand, what if he wasn't?

His eyelids closed ever so sexy. She couldn't believe he would kiss her when he told her about manning up and not bothering her. Her stomach tingled with excitement. She closed her eyes.

Their bodies meshed into each other as his full lips ascended on her. Stimulating shivers swirled down her back. His right hand brushed her hair, and he gently ran his fingers along the back of her neck, making her automatically give a soft moan. Her mouth shivered as his lips pressed against hers and a warm, loving feeling filled her as the kiss ended.

He gave her a gaze which nearly stopped her heart. "I'll call you tomorrow. Our evening ended too short. I wanted to talk to you about something."

"Okay." She wanted to say more. Her head spun. If he was seeing Kim, why'd he kissed her so passionately? Was it perhaps a good-bye kiss?

Later, Melody slipped into bed between freshly washed sheets, smelling lemony from fabric softener. She wondered what Jordan wanted to talk about. Surely Kim, she decided. Maybe everything was okay. Maybe he wanted to say he saw Kim for business purposes only. With the thought, she fell into a deep slumber.

The next day, Jordan called in the morning. "I'm on my way to work. I wanted to check with you to see if you'd like to enjoy a late afternoon comedy movie. Do you still like them?"

She giggled. "Absolutely, I love them more than ever."

"Then we could have dinner afterwards, and I can tell you what's on my mind."

She heard him take a heavy sigh.

She brushed a hand through her hair. She longed to find out what was going on: Was he in love with Kim? Or did she have a second chance with Jordan? "Do you want to talk about it now? Get it off your chest?"

"No, I'd better get to work. We're still working on the case that came up last night. We should finish this morning. The captain says I can take off work after lunch. I'd better go now. Bye."

"Good-bye."

Hours later, Melody looked at her attire: a blue, two-piece, rayon dress with a cowl neckline. The outfit was a favorite and, perhaps, too fancy for a movie, but she was in a good mood at the thought she may have a second chance with Jordan. So she dressed up.

Picking up a hair brush, she finished twirling her long hair into a twisted, French knot. She applied some pink blush and lipstick and put on a set of tiny silver earrings. She slipped into a pair of blue sandals.

At the movie, Melody laughed with Jordan at the comedy plot until her stomach hurt. Afterwards, they drove to an Italian restaurant in Krebs, a tiny community several miles south of McAlester.

Inside, they sat at a small table, covered with a white linen tablecloth, in a room for two.

A waitress brought them their drinks and a platter of cheese, olives and peppers.

"What would the two of you like?" she asked.

Jordan raised his eyebrows and smiled at Melody. "What interests you?"

Melody smiled. "I'd like the Italian dinner."

Jordan looked at the waitress. "Make it two Italian dinners, please."

The server wrote down their orders on her notepad and nodded. "I'll bring your salads out."

"Thanks," Jordan and Melody said at the same time.

The waitress stepped out and returned with a bowl of lettuce greens, mixed with an oil and vinegar dressing. "Anything else I can get you for now?"

"Not for me." Melody looked at Jordan.

"I'm good too."

He nodded at the waitress.

"Very well." She left the two of them alone.

Melody eased in her chair. "How's your police work coming?"

He took a bite of salad. "Good. We finished our case today. It involved a couple arrests on juveniles. I can't give you their names. We're obligated to keep kid's names quiet from the media."

"Of course. I understand the policy. Jordan, I'm so proud of you. You're so good at your police work. I'm so relieved Sonny and Leo are behind bars again."

"And so am I. Don't give me all the credit though. Remember, my units I worked with helped, like you."

"Still, you remind me so much of my father."

"That's a great compliment," he said. "Thank you."

Just then the waitress came with bowls of spaghetti and meatballs and spiced bread.

The server left them alone again.

They engaged in light conversation as they ate their dinners.

When they finished, Jordan scooted his chair forward. "Melody, about your father…I don't know how to tell you this."

"Yes, what did you want to say?" She leaned forward.

He shook his head. "I did something terrible."

She raised her eyebrows. "What on earth is it?"

He let out a deep breath and took her hands. She felt them tremble.

She smiled. "It's okay. Go ahead. Tell me."

He blew out a breath. "Whew! This is a lot harder than I'd even realized it would be."

The sadness and fear in his eyes melted her heart. She took his hands and held them tight. "Just tell me. It'll be okay."

"I wish I knew that for sure. My future depends on what I'm about to tell you. You may not want to see me again, after I give you the details on your father's death. And, if you don't, I understand, even if it will break my heart. I love you."

"How wonderful! I love you too, Jordan."

He jerked his head. "Really?"

"Yes, I've fallen in love with you all over again, or maybe I never fell out of love with you." She looked at him. "Now that really doesn't matter; does it? Not as long as you're interested in Kim."

He frowned. "Kim?"

She released her hands from his and wiped her palms on her skirt. "Yes, Kim. Bill and I saw your car parked by hers a week ago at Cozy Diner. And you even told me you'd been seeing her."

His face softened. "I'm not interested in Kim romantically."

"You're not?" Her heart beat hard at the information.

"No, she was our informant for the big drug bust."

Melody gasped. "Oh my, I've got a confession. I'm afraid I've been terribly jealous. So, that's why you and the captain were so secretive when I asked about her?"

"Exactly."

Melody laughed as tears streamed down her face. "Perfect!"

She retrieved a handkerchief from her purse and wiped the tears off her face.

He leaned forward. "Now, I've got to tell you about your father."

He gently took her hands. How wonderful they felt to her.

"I'm the one responsible for your father's death."

"What?" Stunned, she kept holding his hands, feeling the masculine warmth surround her. "I'm afraid I don't have a clue what you're talking about."

"Of course you don't. I never mentioned it before."

Melody wanted Jordan to explain. She wouldn't rush him. She could see from his face that what he was about to tell her was going to be hard for him. She would give him the time he needed.

"I don't know if you will ever forgive me. Remember how your father was killed with one police unit in one house, while I was in a different house with other law enforcement during the raid?"

"Of course, I remember. I'll never forget it. You were really brave during the raid. You shot one of the biggest drug dealers in Oklahoma."

Jordan held up his hands. "Stop right there. I don't deserve credit. I should have been in the building with your father."

Melody frowned. "I'm afraid I don't understand."

"Well, originally, I was scheduled to go with his unit. I asked Captain Scott if I could go to the other house with the other unit. I figured we'd have a better chance of capturing everyone we needed to that way."

Melody kept frowning, trying to figure out what Jordan was getting at. "And, no doubt, you did. Everyone involved in selling drugs was captured in the raid."

Jordan leaned forward across the table.

"If I'd been with your father, he'd still be living."

Melody heard the quiver in his voice. "Why would you say such a thing?"

"Because I could have saved his life."

"How?"

"By shooting the man who shot him first."

"You have no way of knowing that. Why, if you weren't in the other house, other officers could have been killed. You're not to blame. I would never feel differently about you because of the situation. You did everything you possibly could."

****

Jordan could hardly believe what he was hearing. "You mean you forgive me then?"

"There's nothing to forgive. You didn't avoid being with my father on purpose. And, even if you were with him, you probably wouldn't have been able to save his life. Captain Scott and other officers were with him. If they couldn't save my father's life, how would you have?"

Jordan shook his head. He honestly never thought about it before. "I'm not sure."

"Sometimes that happens. Lieutenant Jordan Lakewater, listen to me. I never once blamed you for my father's death, and I never will."

For the first time, Jordan felt relief dissolve from his body, like a swift wind. An elation entered his soul, a comfort he couldn't explain. All the guilt he'd carried in his heart over the last few years evaporated.

She took his hands. "I understand police work."

He grinned. "You'd make some policeman a wonderful wife."

****

Heart pounding, she smiled. "I've been thinking about that."

"Oh?" Jordan's eyebrows raised. "What? I'm all ears."

"I think I've found the policeman I want."

Jordan's dark eyes widened. "Miss O'Brien, are you proposing to me?"

Melody burst into laughter. "Yes, I guess I am! Do you still want me to marry you?"

"Melody, darling, of course I'll marry you! I still have the ring I bought for you."

"You saved it?" The information surprised her.

"Yes. I was going to sell it. I just couldn't. I couldn't bear to part with it. I know it sounds silly, but I kept it on my bedroom dresser. I never got over you. I realize it now. I also know how clear you made things. You said you could never marry someone in law enforcement."

Melody's heart beat rapidly, not from fear, from excitement at the thought she was just given a second chance with Jordan.

The waitress opened the door. "How is everything? Can I get you anything else?"

Still holding hands, Jordan glanced up at her. "She just proposed and I said yes."

The waitress smiled knowingly. "Very well, sir. I'm bringing you both some cheesecake for dessert to celebrate. My treat."

Epilogue
One year later

In the bridal room of a country church near McAlester, Melody looked in the full-length mirror. Her gown featured a scooped U-neckline in front and back with a tight fitting and sleeveless bodice, covered in sequins. A chiffon overlay fell over the fully gathered, floor length, satin skirt. Carefully, she lifted her waist-length veil to place over her long-styled curls. A sparkling crown set on top of the veil.

Kim and Aunt Sharon helped her fluff the sheer net fabric into place.

Melody turned to her sister-in-law to be. "What do you think? Do I look okay?"

Alexandria smiled. "You glow with radiance. Wait until my brother sees you. He's going to flip out. I'm so thrilled over this wedding. You and my brother were meant for each other."

Kim picked up two small bouquets of white roses and babies' breath which matched two large floral arrangements, setting on a table. "You look fantastic."

Kim handed Alexandria one of the small bouquets.

"Thanks," Alexandria said.

Sharon clicked her tongue. "Melody, you're one beautiful bride. Oh, goodness. I'm so happy I'm going to cry, and I wasn't going to, at least not until after the wedding."

Melody hugged her aunt. "It's all right. You can cry

if you want to." She backed up and studied her aunt, wearing a floor length, two-piece, pink, satin dress with a small pink hat and short veil. "You make a beautiful bride too, auntie."

"I'm so glad we decided on a double wedding. Thank you, dear."

Melody laughed. "What're you thanking me for?"

"For giving me the courage to propose to Bill. Why, I never dreamed I'd do the proposing. Then I realized a woman can do such a thing these days. And, after you told me about the way you proposed to Jordan this time, I got up my courage."

Everyone laughed.

Alexandria patted Sharon's shoulder. "From what I understand, Bill was quick to accept."

Sharon giggled like a child as she held a white gloved hand to her mouth. "Actually, yes. He said he'd wanted to propose a few months after we'd been having coffee together and going to social events this past year, but he didn't have the nerve. Why, if I'd waited for him to pop the question, I might still be a widow. I'm looking so forward to our life together."

"Bill's a dear, just like Jordan." Melody looked at her aunt.

Kim agreed as she ran her fingers down her pink, satin dress, designed the same as Sharon's attire. "I'm thrilled for both of you, and I'm pleased to be your maid-of-honor."

"And, I'm thrilled to be your bridesmaid," Alexandria said. She wore the same styled dress as Kim, only it was a two-piece maternity dress.

"Thanks, all of you. You're such special people in my life." Melody embraced them and chuckled. "If we don't stop with the hugs, I'm going to cry too."

"Now, my niece told me tears are a great blessing and she's right." Sharon dabbed her eyes with a tissue from a box setting on a nearby table. She looked in the mirror. "Could someone freshen up my makeup?"

"Of course." Picking up a small bottle of liquid cream, Kim applied the appropriate touches to Sharon's face. "There. How do you like it?"

Sharon looked in the mirror. "Great. Thanks."

Just then a woman, with short, dark hair, peeked into the room.

"Melody, I wanted to come in to wish you the best. I won't stay long. Everyone's gathered upstairs. Bill and Jordan look so happy. Their suit seams are about to burst."

Melody gazed at her about to be mother-in-law. "Mrs. Lakewater—"

"Please, call me Mom. Welcome to the family. I couldn't ask for a more wonderful daughter-in-law."

"Mom, I can't thank you enough for being here. Jordan's so happy about you joining AA and turning your life around."

"So am I, dear." She glanced at her daughter. "Alexandria and Jordan have been so supportive. So has their father." She turned to Melody. "By the way, dear, my husband's thrilled about getting a daughter-in-law. He loves you like I do."

"I can't wait to have all of you over for family outings," Melody said.

"It'll be such fun," Sharon smiled.

Mrs. Lakewater hugged Melody. In the middle of the embrace, Melody's veil almost fell off.

Jordan's mother quickly stepped back and

rearranged the net fabric. "I'm so sorry. I didn't mean to mess things up."

"You didn't," Melody quickly pointed out as she straightened the veil.

"Well, I'd better go. You both make beautiful brides. I'm so excited!" Jordan's mother exited the room.

Aunt Sharon looked at Melody. "Jordan's parents are going to be such a nice addition to the family."

"I totally agree." She picked up the large bouquets from the table and handed one to her aunt. "Ready?"

"Absolutely." Sharon took the flowers.

Upstairs, Alexandria and then Kim marched slowly down the aisle. Next the bridal song began. Melody and her aunt strolled, side by side, as they headed toward the altar. The packed crowd stood and turned to the brides.

Quickly, Melody glanced at the stained windows. Late afternoon sunlight poured through the windows, sending an array of colored light over the congregation. Aunt Sharon walked right beside her as she glanced at everyone, flooded in the colored light. She looked at her soon-to-be husband. My, he looked handsome in his tux.

With a wide smile, she gazed at him through her veil. He stood tall, erect and grinned like there was no tomorrow.

So did Bill.

Melody winked at Jordan. She couldn't have been happier. In her heart, she knew she was ready to be a policeman's wife.

A word about the author...

Award-winning author, Mary Ann Kerl grew up on a family farm near Glenham, South Dakota. At the age of nine, she moved with her parents and two brothers to a small town, Herreid, where she graduated high school. She then attended South Dakota State University and began her studies in Journalism and Family Consumer Science.

Three days after college graduation, she married Bob Kerl, also an SDSU alumni. The two made their first home in Newport News, Virginia. Before settling in McAlester, Oklahoma, where they still reside, they also lived in Texas and Alabama, since Bob was in the military. When he served in Viet Nam, Mary Ann resided in Portland, Oregon. She loves the fact that she experienced living on both the east and west coast and the north and south regions of the United States, because she enjoys meeting people. Mary Ann and Bob have two grown sons and three grandchildren.

Mary Ann sold 16 books to traditional, royalty-paying publishers, including Augsburg and Honor Books. Double Danger marks her first suspense book. She loves writing in this genre. She has published books, articles and short stories for all ages, from toddlers to senior citizens. She sold over 2,000 articles and short stories to over 100 publishers, including *Jack and Jill, Children's Digest, Home Life, Family Circle, The Writer, Writer's Digest* and others. She has received over 50 writing awards.

For nearly twenty years, she worked as a newspaper correspondent, first for *Tulsa World* and then for *The Daily Oklahoman*, the two largest papers in the state. Her educational credits include a doctoral degree in E-learning. She has taught journalism, communication and English courses for college students as well as English and creative writing for middle and high schoolers.

Presently, she is working on another suspense book for adults and a contemporary novel for middle-graders. Her hobbies are cooking, sewing, reading, taking walks, playing the piano, going to the movies and enjoying her grandchildren.

Mary Ann received an award in the contemporary romance category for *Double Danger* in an annual Oklahoma Writer's Federation, Inc. contest.

https://makoklahoma.wixsite.com/mysite-4

Thank you for purchasing
this publication of The Wild Rose Press, Inc.

For questions or more information
contact us at
info@thewildrosepress.com.

The Wild Rose Press, Inc.
www.thewildrosepress.com

www.ingramcontent.com/pod-product-compliance
Lightning Source LLC
Chambersburg PA
CBHW070452260626
47161CB00004B/1278